Rose's Nightmare Returns

Phyllis A. Collmann

ISBN: 978-1-57579-412-9

Library of Congress Control Number: 2009932995

First printing 2009
Second printing 2013

For additional copies of this or other
books written by Phyllis Collmann:
pac51@hickorytech.net
712-552-2375
www.collmannwarehouse.com

Printed in the United States of America

PINE HILL PRESS
4000 West 57th Street
Sioux Falls, SD 57106

Dedication

To my husband, Colin,
for 61 years of marriage and for his
devoted love and support.

To my children
Cynthia, Kimberly, Ronald and Melonie.
I love you dearly.

To my grandchildren
and great grandchildren.
I love each one special.

❧ About the Author ❧

Phyllis A. Collmann is a retired nurse. She lives on a farm in northwest Iowa, with her husband of 61 years. While living on the same farm for 50 years, she continues to write about the Rose Donlin series. This is the sixth book in the series and is a sequel to her first, second, third, fourth, and fifth pioneer books. The first book is called *Rose's Betrayal and Survival*. The second book is called *Rose's Triumphant Return* and the third is called *Rose's Heart's Decision*. The fourth book is called *Rose's Dream Fulfilled* and the fifth book is called *Rose's Unexpected Tragedy*.

Published books:
  Rose's Betrayal and Survival
  Rose's Triumphant Return
  Rose's Heart's Decision
  Rose's Dream Fulfilled
  Rose's Unexpected Tragedy
  Rose's Nightmare Returns

  Kim's Unplanned Sega
  Mother's Innocence Proven
  Christmas At Our House

A Very Special Thank You

Julie Ann Madden
Diane Ten Napel
Kimberly Ann Bonnett

❧ *Chapter* 1 ❧

Wiley Rineheart was not a man who took orders well. He did not like to be told what to do. He was more like Wilber Kolveck than he wanted anyone to know.

They had grown-up together. The play time always ended up in a fight with Wilber's sister, Dora, trying to separate them. Wilber would beg and plead with Dora to hit Wiley for him.

While they were playing Wilber needed to win or he became angry and always out of control. He would bite and usually draw blood before he would release the hold with his teeth. Wilber was heavier and stronger. Dora always took care of the wound.

Now, he was here asking for help!

Wiley was silent and stood with his arms crossed over his chest, looking directly at Wilber. His mind drifted back and the old painful feelings came back. This would be very difficult for him. Wiley guessed Wilber had done something bad.

The two families drifted apart after Wiley's mother could see Wilber appeared to have something wrong with him. She thought of him as a misfit. Years later would prove her right. He had become a recluse with a worse temper than he had as a child.

Wiley remembered her telling him, "I will not stand by and watch Wilber Kolveck beat you up." His mother loved her sister but this was not acceptable. Her son came first.

Finally, Wiley took a deep breath and said, "You can stay in the wood shed out behind my mother's house. I'll bring you water to drink and food each day. You are allowed to go out only after dark. No one must see you. I'll come out when my mother is asleep."

Wiley would definitely not want his mother to know Wilber Kolveck was living in her wood shed. Dora had been the one she really liked but each time she saw Dora, Wilber had been with her. So, Mrs. Rineheart had not seen Dora for many years.

∝ Chapter 2 ∝

Now, Wilber was going to live the life that Henry Helgens had lived for seven months.

Wiley stopped talking for a few seconds, then added, "Do you understand?"

Wilber had no one else to ask for help or anyone to hide him. He knew from the sound of Wiley Rineheart's voice, in which he felt he heard distaste, anger, and resentment. But this was his only way to hide, and this would be the time to plan his next attempt to find a way to get to Henry Helgens or one of Henry's family. Nothing would stop him because in his mind he thought everyone was against him and he was blameless. Wilber had lost reality.

Wilber did not tell Wiley anything he had done recently, nor did he tell him any connection he had had with Henry and Rose Donlin Helgens.

⬿ Chapter 3 ⬾

Wiley's mother and Wilber's mother were sisters. The families spent a lot of time together. At first it was fun for the little boys playing together, but as time past and they grew older, Wilber began to act different.

He no longer played fair. The need to be first or best was the only way he would play. Dora tried to cover up for him. She would separate them and explain to Wiley, he didn't mean it. Wilber became annoying and at the same time he teased Wiley, mistreated him and showed him no kindness.

Wilber had no idea he acted rude and uncivilized. At the end of a play time, Wiley always had cuts and bruises.

Wilber's parents found caring for him becoming more difficult. They pushed most of the care on Dora. She would calm him down or she would take him to the kitchen and feed him whatever he asked for. This became a pattern. He grew heavier and clumsier.

It was after Wilber's parents talked about sending him to be confined in an institution after agreeing they no longer could care for him. Dora took complete care of him.

⬿ Chapter 4 ⬾

Dora prepared his breakfast before school because he always ended up tipping his bowl over on the table or dropping his bowl on the floor. She would patiently clean the kitchen up after him so their mother would not see it in a mess. Every morning was the same.

His skills at dressing did not improve. When Dora realized his mismatched clothes meant nothing to him, she started laying his clothes out on the back of a chair each night before going to bed. She washed one set of clothing by hand each night.

After Dora had scolded him every morning for a very long time and threatened to take all of his clothes into her bedroom, he began to wear the clothing she picked out for him. Each morning he walked into the kitchen with his shirt buttoned up wrong and he could not tie his shoes. He had been told how and shown every morning since he was small.

Dora insisted he go to the outhouse before they left for school. She would whisper to him at their lunch break to go out behind the school to the outhouse. The teacher complained to Dora he was going out behind the school, but not out to the outhouse. So again, Dora made him walk with her to the outhouse. Sometimes she had to push him in front of her.

∽ Chapter 5 ∾

He disrupted the country school classroom, getting up and walking to Dora's desk whenever he wanted to and standing there looking at her. Finally, the teacher put Wilber next to her. Dora tried not to show how angry she felt, but she was his one and only friend.

School and learning was what made Dora happy. Everyone in the classroom knew Dora was a student scholar. In the evening Dora spent hours helping him with his school work but the next day he acted as if he had not studied the evening before at all.

The teacher always called on Dora to answer her questions because she was sure Dora would know the answer. Each time Dora stood up to answer a question, Wilber would also stand up. He felt good about himself and always stood with a smile on his face. Dora's face turned red in embarrassment. Wilber was not aware the kid's snickering was because of him. Dora knew he was being made fun of but Wilber did not.

When Dora was told to step up to the chalk board, Wilber stood up proudly and walked up to the chalk board behind her. He would pick up a piece of chalk and proceed to write on the chalk board.

Dora continued caring for him. Always making sure he was safe and always protecting him from bullies at school.

Dora dreaded lunch time. Wilber's eating skills were grabbing his food in both hands and filling his mouth until his cheeks puffed out. He always made a scene, ending up, coughing. This was one of the times Dora thought her love for Wilber was turning into hate for him. But each day was the same, at the end of the day she continued to watch over him, afraid he would be sent away.

The kids shouted bad things at him after school, and Dora hurried him away from the school. She would close the door of the big white house, relieved to be inside and stop the harshness and dislike everyone felt against Wilber.

∽ *Chapter 6* ∾

Nothing ever seemed to change in Dora's life until Wilber threatened her when he heard about the man named Henry Helgens.

Dora had searched everywhere she thought he could be hiding, and each night drove her team of horses home. After unhitching them from the wagon, she fed and watered the two horses. She walked slowly from the barn and into the big white house feeling terribly lonely.

Wilber had never done anything like this before. She walked passed the bedroom that she and Wilber had kept Henry Helgens a prisoner in.

Of course, she had realized the minute Wilber wanted to save Henry and keep him so he would have a friend, it was a mistake. But, she only wanted Wilber to be happy. Now, she regretted the whole horrible seven months they had taken from Henry's life.

Getting up in the morning for Dora meant dressing, washing her face, and then making her bed. In the kitchen she made a fire in the cook stove. The stove had been in the same spot as far back as she could remember. She cooked her oatmeal the same every morning. The oatmeal was always dry. It looked and tasted exactly like she had prepared Henry Helgens' breakfast for seven long months.

Dora sat at the same table, on the same chair and at the same place at the table. Wishing she had someone to talk to, she laid her face on her arms on the table.

A vision came into her mind and she wondered why this person whom she had not seen or talked to in many years, then Dora remembered why. It had to do with Wilber's temper and his shameful disgrace he put upon the family.

∽ Chapter 7 ∾

Dora left her bowl on the table and headed to the barn to hitch up the team. She knew exactly where she was going. Talking to her aunt seemed the right thing to do.

The ride took over two hours, and Dora was not aware of the scenery nor did she look at anyone. The sun was straight up when she arrived at the Rinehearts' home.

The path into the driveway had weeds growing everywhere. It was hard to tell where to leave the horses. Dora pulled up in front of the house. She tied her team to a couple of posts. She thought this was not how she remembered her Aunt Olive Rineheart's home looked when she was young.

Walking up to the house, Dora watched the curtain on the door move. Then as her hand reached out to knock, she heard the latch click and the door opened.

Olive Rineheart's eyes were studying Dora's face closely.

Then she eagerly reached out, recognizing her niece she had not seen for a very long time. She opened her arms and encircled Dora. The hug was needed by both.

Dora had no idea how much her aunt needed Dora, as much as Dora needed her.

∽ Chapter 8 ∾

Aunt Olive's home looked the same. A picture came into Dora's mind of what it looked like when she was young. Now, it was dark and dingy. The curtains were dirty and hung loosely to the floor. It was dark in the room. The age of Aunt Olive and her home had caught up with her. The toll of years was present. Her beauty was gone. She no longer could care for her beautiful huge home.

Aunt Olive offered Dora coffee and asked her to sit at her kitchen table. Then Olive realized she needed to bring in some wood to heat the stove up to cook the coffee.

Dora offered to help her bring in the wood from the wood shed from behind her home. They walked hand in hand, feeling happy over being reunited. Aunt Olive opened the wood shed's locked door.

Dora stepped in, leaned down to gather up as many chunks of wood as she could carry. Aunt Olive did the same but could carry only half as much. They both carefully stepped out into the clear air. Aunt Olive locked the door and they appeared to be glad to draw in a deep clean breath of air into their bodies. The odor was rancid of mice and rats droppings.

What they did not see or were not aware of, was, in the back of the wood shed, someone was hiding. He lay on the damp cold ground under a black, dirty, heavy canvas. He was cold, hungry, and mad at everyone.

Wiley had promised Wilber a blanket and more food. But, Wiley had not kept his promise. Wilber was also having to keep the rats and mice off of him. They also made their home in the wood pile. Suddenly Wilber woke up to find a rat or mouse climbing on him. Now, Wilber's only thought was to get even.

Chapter 9

Dora drank her coffee and talked about her life with Wilber since both of her parents had passed away. She tried hard not to encourage Aunt Olive to hate Wilber more.

Aunt Olive sat quietly and listened. After Dora had poured her heart out, Aunt Olive invited her to come and live with her and Wiley. Dora heard what Aunt Olive said but did not answer.

"It will be so nice to have another woman in my house." Aunt Olive said so sincerely. "Wiley is not someone you can sit down and visit with; he's very busy in his oil drilling office."

Dora thought it would be nice to have a woman to talk to, but now, she needed to find Wilber before he did something horrible to one of the Helgens' family.

Chapter 10

Dora left feeling she now had made up for the years of separation of her family. It had been a good day for her and she had not had a good day for a very long time.

She had not found Wilber, but now she could start again in the early morning. Taking care of her team was always first. A good night sleep was what she needed.

The following morning was the same as usual. Then she noticed something was missing. Wilber's coat was not hanging on the hook by the kitchen door. She almost ran to his room;

she noted his quilt was not on his bed. Nothing else was missing from his room.

Dora had not been afraid for a long, long time but now she was feeling a dreaded feeling. What if?

Quickly hurrying upstairs and searching through every bedroom, then opening every closet door, and peering in-between her parents clothing and around old hat boxes, she found nothing disturbed.

The basement was dark, dusty and damp but she knew it too had to be looked through. Fifty years of storage-old trunks, clothes, papers, nothing had been wasted or thrown out. Being frugal was a way of life for the Kolveck family. It had paid off, Dora and Wilber were wealthy.

Dora was finding out money was not the answer to everything, especially Wilber's possible sickness. She loved him. She wanted so badly to help him, but first she would have to find him. And she knew she needed to hurry.

✂ Chapter 11 ✄

Rose woke feeling anxious over the children being forced to remain in the house another day. They were getting very restless and agitated at times throughout the day. Inga was working hard to keep them entertained. She read their books to them over and over.

Paul ate part of his lunch only after being begged. He immediately raised his arms wanting to get out of his chair. He stood at the window and watched the men ride out to check the cow herd. And then he watched as the dog Pal ran around in a circle trying to catch his tail. Rose stood watching him and then heard him laugh out loud.

She thought for a few minutes and decided while Inga put the girls down for an afternoon nap she would let Paul run out in the yard for only a short time.

The knock at the front door took her mind off of Paul. She opened the front door to find Mary standing their looking worried. Her eyes looked red, her hair not combed.

Mary spoke first before Rose could say hello.

"Rose, Hank is sick, and I'm thinking I need to put him in the hospital."

Mary then ran to her buggy where Elizabeth sat holding Hank. Sarah sat next to Elizabeth with her head on Hank's lap, so afraid of what was happening.

Rose closed the door needing to lean on it. No one knew about Hank but she and Blue Sky. Nothing bad could be wrong with Hank. If Hank was sick with something that needed his real family's medical past, this would unravel a hidden secret that Rose had hoped she could keep for a very long, long time. Now she felt doubt.

Mary and her two daughters were living in Missouri. They were living in a cabin with an abusive husband and father named Jessie Rocker. Rose and Henry met them one evening while they were traveling to Oklahoma City. Henry and Rose stopped at Jessie's homestead to ask if they could rest the night in his barn. Jessie had been drinking all day. He had insisted they eat supper and spend the evening in his cabin. Jessie was rude and mean to his wonderful family.

Mary had begged Henry to take her and her daughters with him. It wasn't until Henry made another trip into Oklahoma City that he brought Mary, Elizabeth, and Sarah with him.

Mary did not know at the time she was expecting another baby of Jessie Rocker.

The baby, Hank that Mary believed to be hers was born to another young woman who passed away giving birth and her baby was stillborn.

Rose and Blue Sky secretly switched the baby boys.

Then Rose heard Paul giggling and squealing. She raced to the back door and found Paul playing with Pal. Relieved she took him into the cabin and washed his face and hands and even with his disapproval, laid him down for his nap.

It wasn't until Paul woke from his nap, he began to talk about the man he had talked to.

Rose was dressed in warm clothing but suddenly her body was cold. Paul loved to play and being nearly two years old meant learning to play hide and seek and scaring his sisters.

This was not a game and he was scaring Rose, was he making this up?

Listening to Paul tell the same story, Rose remained calm and quiet. Henry heard the story while putting his son to bed that night. It was the same story Paul told his mother.

"Man down on his belly on other side wire. He not big man like you father," Paul said as he put his little head down on his pillow.

Henry hurried to ask Paul, "What color coat was this little man wearing?"

"Pink," Paul answered.

Henry stood and watched as his little boy closed his eyes and went to sleep.

Rose and Henry sat at the kitchen table discussing the afternoon wondering if this was all a small boy's imagination. After all, he had heard everyone talking about the little man.

Chapter 12

Rose could not get to sleep; her mind was not only on Wilber Kolveck but Mary's baby Hank. She slipped out of bed as Henry's breathing was steady and even. She did not want to alert anyone; she ran the four miles to Blue Sky's cabin. Rose tapped on the door. Blue Sky unlatched the lock and showed surprise on her face.

"Blue Sky, you must go to the hospital and help Mary's Hank," Rose said with a sound of worry.

The two women looked deep into each other's eyes. Nothing more was said. Blue Sky pulled her best friend close until her arms encircled Rose and held her close. Blue Sky released her slowly.

"Rose," Blue Sky said, "your color looks pale, do you want to tell me some thing?"

"We'll talk when Hank is better." Rose said, knowing Blue Sky already knew.

Chapter 13

"Wiley, please get rid of the rats and mice in the wood shed. Because if you don't, I'm going to shoot them myself." Olive Rineheart's voice sounded angry.

He had been paying no attention to her. Now, he was listening.

She went on to say, "The canvas moved when I went to bring wood in this morning."

He took a deep breath and said loudly, "I'll take care of the wood shed; you just stay out of there."

⚛ Chapter 14 ⚛

Wilber lay awake under the dirty canvas after his long walk. The sparrows were waking and starting their morning ritual. Fluttering their wings and flying in and out of the small hole in the window pane. He could hear small droppings on the canvas coming from the sparrows. The corners of the ceiling were filled with bird nests, left there from year to year. The air was full of dust and feathers. Breathing for Wilber was becoming painful.

He decided to stay in the wood shed until the afternoon, and then go see his new little friend. He had a wooded area he would travel through. No one would ever find him.

Wilber had worked very hard for two nights kicking the lower three boards from the back of the corner post. He could squeeze through by pushing the boards out as far as it took so his awkward body could get through. Getting back in the wood shed was always difficult. The nails caught on his clothes and he would lose his temper each attempt he made. When he was finally able to crawl into the shed, he would reach down and pull back the boards back tightly to the post. No one knew, not even Wiley.

∽ Chapter 15 ∾

Wiley's day had been long and the meeting he had had with Henry Helgens took up most of his afternoon. One of the oil wells needed a new part and Henry felt Wiley's Oil Company should pay for it because it had only worked a few hours. But Wiley had argued until Henry gave in and paid an exuberant price for it. When Henry was out the door and the door was closed, Wiley had a big smile on his face.

∽ Chapter 16 ∾

Wilber felt warm with his coat on even if it was buttoned wrong. He would wrap his quilt around him under the canvas. The sparrows were all flying back in while all of the babies were chirping. The sounds were extremely loud. Wilber pulled the canvas down enough to see the mother sparrows feeding their hungry babies.

Then a sound from over head, above the shed sounded like thunder and then Wilber could hear rain hitting the roof. This was too much. Water was dripping down on him from the leaky roof. His clothes were becoming wet, and he was shivering from the cold.

He decided then he needed to find somewhere else to hide. Somewhere near the Rose and Henry Helgens' homestead, but hidden enough so no one could find him.

He pressed his feet firmly against the loose bottom boards. The boards began to move ever so slightly. He pushed his feet out first. The rain had made the ground into mud but he continued to work until his body was out of the wood shed. His shoes were muddy as was all of his clothing and the rain was soaking through his clothing to his skin. He replaced the boards by sticking the nails back into the post. No one could tell he had been there.

After many tries he staggered up onto his feet, looked around and could not see or recognize any place in any direction because of the torrential rain fall.

Wilber walked to the back of the wood shed. He stood up against it to get the right direction he needed to go in. He knew where he wanted to go. He just didn't know how to get there.

The heavy rain was making it difficult to go in one direction. It was so easy to turn and try to find a way to get out of the rain. When he finally came to a tree area, he found a large tree for shelter with branches leaning close to the ground. He squatted under it.

In the early morning Aunt Olive was up early. She dressed quietly so not to wake Wiley. She had not used her husband's shotgun since he had died. This early morning she was going to use it. The day before she had cleaned the gun and loaded it. The door opened with no squeak. The walk to the wood shed was in the dark. The path was wet and when she got to the wood shed the rain drops were dripping off the roof. It was truly an act of desperation. Once inside she lowered the gun and blasted at the canvas. The gun nearly knocked her down on to the wood pile.

She staggered back a couple of steps. The smell of the combination of gun smoke, wet canvas, wet bird feathers and a dirty wood shed was a terrible stink.

Wiley heard the gun shot. It took him only seconds to get to the wood shed because of the terror in his heart.

He yelled, "Mother, did you kill-- and then he stopped. "What did you shoot at? What Mother, what?"

"I shot at the rats under the canvas," she said in a very defensive voice.

Wiley turned and ran back to the house to get a lantern. With the lantern in hand, he stepped into the wood shed and took steps to the back and looked down at a canvas filled with holes from gun pellets.

He leaned down with a vision of seeing Wilber filled with buckshot. Lifting a corner of the canvas, he saw only the ground. He continued to lift it higher and suddenly he realized Wilber was not there. Wilber was gone.

Wilber woke just before dawn. The rain was falling gently now, and he was wet, cold and needing to find something to eat.

The forest area he had traveled in most of the day was exactly where he wanted to go. He traveled many miles around the Rose Donlin Helgens' homestead. He wanted to remember it all. He would spend a lot of time watching until the time was right.

He did not want anyone to see him. He would have liked to have seen his new little friend, but not today. He headed for an old run-down cabin he had seen when he was watching Henry Helgens many months before.

He snuck into the corral first and hid in a stall under some old dry hay. He burrowed down under the hay as far as he could. The relief was overwhelming. Wilber had reached his new home. He knew he would have to move again, but this time it would be to the barn. He would wait for darkness before moving up into the haymow.

∽ Chapter 17 ∾

While he laid waiting, he heard a scratching noise; he did not move. The sound was coming closer. Then he felt some pressure on his legs and a pecking through the dry hay. He was lying on his back while the pecking was coming closer to his face. He felt a sharp stick on his chest, and the pain was starting to hurt and also made him furious. Before he could turn over or reach up out of the hay he was pecked again. This time on his neck and the pain was getting worse. With no hesitation, he reached up and grabbed the neck of an old red rooster. He sat up straight and with all the strength he had, he threw the poor unsuspecting fowl across the corral. The rooster hit the wall and lay quiet for a few minutes then stood up on wobbly legs, ruffled his feathers and strutted off as if nothing had happened. He happened to be the same rooster that attacked Rose Donlin when she had first arrived here eight years earlier. His eyes were blurry now. The rooster's spurs were like weapons, long knife sharp and he wandered the homestead.

Climbing the ladder that was 15 feet straight up to the haymow was not easy for Wilber. He was also afraid and breathing loudly. When he reached the wooden floor, he lay flat trying to get his breath. Finally, he was able to get up on his knees, and then stand up. He climbed over the hay to the back of the haymow to find a place to hide.

∼ Chapter 18 ∼

The noise from a wagon and horses coming down the road woke Wilber. He quietly peeked out between the dried old barn boards. His eyes strained to see who was driving the team of mules. When his eyes adjusted, he stared at the big black man driving the team. He had not seen him when he was here before. He sat back down in his hiding place and thought about how large the black man was. He had never seen a black man before.

Something else was bothering him, too. He had not eaten for two days. He also needed a drink of water. It couldn't get dark soon enough. When it was dark, Wilber's concern was getting down the steep ladder and out of the barn. His foot slipped off of the wooden rung three steps up and he fell hard to the dirt floor of the barn. He lay stunned for a few minutes before getting up.

His foot and leg hurt as he made his way to the creek for a long drink of water. On his way back to the barn, he stopped at a small building attached to the cabin. He unlatched the door. It was the smokehouse. It had a slab of smoked meat hanging on a hook. He felt around hoping to find a knife to cut a piece of meat off. He opened the door a few inches and he could see a knife lying on a bench. The piece of meat he sliced off would last him a couple of days. It had been smoked so he could eat it now.

Wilber decided he would make the trip to the creek each night after dark and when his meat was gone, he would also stop at the smokehouse.

The next morning he watched while he sat on his knees as the black man walked toward the barn. He continued to watch as the large black man drove his team up the road.

He was beginning to feel pain in his foot and leg from the fall off of the ladder the night before. Wilber began thinking about Dora. She always helped him but he was sure she would not help him with his pain now.

⌒ *Chapter 19* ⌒

Mary arrived at the hospital with her sick baby. Not knowing why her son Hank had suddenly stopped eating and his body felt warmer than normal. His cough had started out a few coughs a day and then the cough got worse, waking him at night. Hank was not sleeping at night, and she was awake most of the night. Now Elizabeth and Sarah were waking when hearing him cough.

Mary's love for her son was the end of an abusive marriage and the beginning of a happy life. She told herself her son was the best part of her husband. She also told herself her son's father Jesse Rocker, had so many reasons he turned out the way he did, but she was determined her son would not live his life like his father had lived his.

How the secret had been kept, Mary did not know.

The nurse opened the door for Mary and Hank. Elizabeth was following her mother with tears in her eyes and holding on to Sarah's hand. Both girls looked worried for their baby brother.

The nurse took Hank into a private room. She stripped him of his clothing and began to sponge him with cool water. His body was covered with red spots. He whimpered and whined in pain.

Blue Sky entered the hospital without anyone hearing her. Her leather knee-high moccasins allowed her to come and go with no noise. Her graceful steps were fast, swift and soft.

She appeared at Hank's room carrying her medical bag. She slipped in next to Mary before being heard. Mary's face and body showed the nights she had not been sleeping. The love Mary had for her son was evident.

Blue Sky gently led Mary to the door and explained she would do all she could for Hank and she would like Mary to take Elizabeth and Sarah to the kitchen for something to eat. Mary obeyed knowing only Blue Sky could help Hank now.

Blue Sky asked the nurse to turn the lamp as low as it would go, but still stay lit. She opened her bag and began mixing green stems and powder with a small amount of water. She mixed it with her fingers, making a dark thick mud pack. Blue Sky worked fast to cover every area of Hank's small body. Hank's whining stopped.

Hank fought at first, but he was weak and tired. Blue Sky asked the nurse to let him suck on a clean cloth soaked in cold water with sugar and a drop of kerosene. He continued to suck on the cloth until he was asleep. He lay that afternoon and night, uncovered with only his mud pack on. He remained in the cool dark room all night.

Blue Sky sent word to Rose asking if any of her renters had goat's milk. Blue Sky needed the milk immediately for Hank.

Rose informed Inga the girls were to stay inside at all times. They could help Inga make bread and cookies. Paul could go out to play for only fifteen minutes in the afternoon before his nap.

❦ Chapter 20 ❧

Rose left in a hurry, mounted on her magnificent horse. She knew the renter's homestead she was going to. The ride was fast, and it felt good to be riding on the horse she loved.

The renter had milked that morning, and the milk was stored in the cold cave. She explained the need for the milk, and the reason to hurry the milk back to the hospital.

Rose arrived at the hospital and entered the kitchen. She told the cook to warm a small amount and keep the remaining portion cold.

Rose walked into Hank's room carrying a small amount of warm goat's milk. The two women's eyes met; neither spoke. Rose tried to hide her frightened feeling when she saw Hank covered with a greenish brown mud pack over his entire body.

He was whining as he began to waken. Blue Sky lifted his head up and then his back enough to be able to drink the warm milk. He drank a full cup and she gently laid him back down asleep. His body lie still as his breathing was quiet and steady.

Rose wanted to hear Blue Sky say, "Hank would recover." But she did not.

Rose started toward the door and turned to Blue Sky and said, "I'll check on my children and come back to help you." Blue Sky heard but did not reply.

↶ *Chapter 21* ↷

Wilber's pain was worsening, and he found a tree limb to lean on so he could walk to the creek for water. The meat from the smoke house was salty making him thirsty.

He decided the limb to lean on was helping. So, he thought he could get through the trees and maybe, his friend would be outside.

Inga laid Margaret and Myra down for their afternoon nap as Rose had told her. Paul stood waiting by the door to the large back yard. Inga opened the door and Paul jumped down off of the last step and ran the entire fence line. The second time around the yard, he suddenly stopped when he saw Wilber lying down flat on his stomach next to the fence. He could not be seen from the cabin as a huge bush was on the outside of the fence, and he was hiding under it.

Wilber was digging a hole under the fence with his hands.

Paul was so happy to see the funny short man he laid down on the inside of the fence across from Wilber. Paul was so fascinated with how fast the man's hands were working. Paul had no idea why the little man was digging this hole. Paul watched as Wilber dug and pushed the dirt out of the hole and moved it to the side.

When Wilber thought he could get Paul out of the yard, he said, "You can get out now. Come on, I'll help you." He talked to Paul softly, so not to scare him. "Put your head through. I'll pull you the rest of the way." Wilber held his breath for the fear of not getting a hold of him.

Paul put his head down and started it through the hole. He stopped, lifted his head back and said, "Baby cows crying. Babies want their mama." Paul loved the cow herd. His father would take him on Rose's magnificent horse to check on the cows each morning when he no longer could play in the back-yard alone.

Paul's head was under the fence and Wilber was overjoyed. He quickly pulled his head back again and said, "I not get out; Mommy will be mad at me."

"No, no she won't care. We can play together in the trees. I know some games we can play." Wilber was trying hard to convince him. He wanted him so badly.

Paul was inching his way to the hole under the fence. His head was just about under when he heard Inga's loud voice coming through the air in her German accent saying, "Paaaaul, Paaaaul, mommys home. You have to come inside."

"Hurry, hurry," Wilber was feeling panic.

Paul wiggled back under the fence, jerked his head back on his side of the fence as quick as he could.

"Mommy home," Paul said as he jumped to his feet and ran toward Inga and the cabin. Paul ran into the kitchen where his mother was getting him a glass of milk before laying him down for his nap.

Paul had left Wilber red-faced and yelling softly, "No, no. Come back."

Wilber refilled the hole and pulled grass and threw it over the dirt so no one could see where he had dug. He limped into the tree area and out of sight of the cabin. He had failed this time but the next time would be different.

∽ Chapter 22 ∾

On the way passed the old Higgins cabin, Wilber opened the smokehouse door. The knife was lying on the bench in the same place. He cut two deep slices of meat and then something caught his eye. It was an old blanket hanging on the wall. Wilber took a painful step closer and with one finger, lifted the blanket. He peered inside of the cabin. He could not have been more surprised.

The cabin was very old, built in 1820. The cabin stood through the strong winds, heavy rains, hot sun and cold ice storms. Joseph Higgins father had built the cabin after he claimed the land. Now the cabin and land belonged to Rose Donlin Helgens. The walls showed all the boards the outside boards were nailed to. The fireplace still had red and orange embers in it. Over the fire a large black wrought iron-pot was hanging. It smelled so good because it had cooked all day for the huge black man's night meal.

Next to the fireplace was a bed with an old patch work quilt covering it. The large square table held a lamp and also a bowl and silverware, ready for the black man's food.

A water pail with a dipper sat on a wooden stand in the corner away from the fireplace.

Wilber grabbed the bowl and spoon from the table and dipped the spoon into the food filling his mouth full. He had not eaten a good meal since he had Henry Helgens taken from him. At that time Dora was doing all of the cooking.

While eating, Wilber looked around for a place to sit down. That's when he noticed a door. Opening the door he stepped into a cold room with a bed, chair and an old trunk. The floor had extra boards pounded over holes in different places to prevent rats, mice, and snakes from coming in.

He sat down on the bed and continued eating all of the food in his bowl. His leg was so painful he thought he would lie down for at least two hours before the black man who lived here would return home. Then he would go to his hiding place in the barn. Wilber covered up with a worn out old quilt. The pain in his leg began to feel less sharp. He had not realized how very painful his foot and leg had been nor how very tired he was. His last thought was if Dora was here, she would take care of him.

The sleep he sank into was deep and dark.

❧ Chapter 23 ❧

Rufus George was coming home after working on Henry and Rose Donlin Helgens homestead. The black man worked long hours.

The oil wells were running smoothly but the amount of oil was overwhelming, and a new wagon was needed to keep up with hauling the oil into Oklahoma City's rail station. Rufus George was an expert at putting the big wagons together. First, lifting the huge heavy boards needed for the wagon and then the big iron wheels. His days were long and tiresome. He worked later and darkness was approaching as he pulled his team into the corral.

He was slower than usual getting the team unhitched, feeding and watering them. Then he walked slowly to the cabin.

Rufus George lit the lamp and went to his wash bowl to wash his hands and face. He went to the table to fill his bowl with the food he was looking forward to eating before going to bed. His bowl was not in the place he had set it in the morning before leaving. The spoon was also missing. He looked in the cast-iron pot and could tell it was not as full as he had left it. The food left was less than half.

He stood for a minute and tried to understand what had happened to his food, bowl and spoon. He looked around for anymore signs of something missing.

Then something caught his eye. The door into the other room was open a small amount. Rufus George reached his hand out with a gentle push of his fingers and quietly opened the door just enough to see into the room. Over the last few years his sight had begun to fade. He blinked a couple of times to make sure he understood what he thought he was seeing.

A body was lying asleep in Rose Donlin's old bed. Rufus George had no idea who it was. He had never seen him before. He stood looking at him wondering what to do.

Wilber stirred and then the unexpected happened, he opened his eyes. He thought his eyes would pop out of his head. He looked into the eyes of the biggest black man he had ever seen. His heart began to race; his skin became clammy. He was trembling with fear all over.

Wilber threw the covers off and tried to get up off of the bed. His good leg was on the floor and then he set the sore leg on the floor expecting to get up. Without any warning, Wilber fell to the floor and cried out in severe pain.

Rufus George moved slowly to Wilber and lifted him easily back up on the bed. Wilber's eyes were open as wide as they had ever been, he was so afraid.

Rufus George spoke first by asking, "ou urt? ["You hurt"].

Wilber was gasping for his breath.

He finally managed to say, "My foot and leg."

Rufus George towered over Wilber lying in the bed. He leaned down and untied Wilber's boot, removing it. The top of his foot and up into his leg was black and blue, mostly black. The boot had rubbed skin off where the foot was swollen.

The other thing Rufus George noticed was how dirty this man looked.

His giant arms slipped under Wilber, lifted him straight up in the air and carried him out of the cabin, grabbing a blanket off of the bed. Also, he picked up two bars of lye soap. He carried Wilber to the creek.

Wilber knew better than try to fight this man who was three times as big as he was.

Once they were to the creek, Rufus George told Wilber, "Aaak oof ur kloos." ["Take off your clothes."] Wilber wasted no time removing everything but his dirty underwear.

Rufus George laid him out straight next to the water on the bank. Wilber would be able to wiggle into the warm water.

Rufus George sat down on the bank and untied his size 18 boots. Wilber lay in the water watching the black man remove the largest boots he'd ever seen a man wear. Then he noticed something else. The scars covering his feet and every toe looked twisted, lapped over the next toe.

Wilber watched as Rufus George stepped into the water with a bar of lye soap and Wilber's dirty clothes. The clothes were all scrubbed with hands covered with scars and then he noticed his thumbs. They were flat as if someone had pounded them with a hammer.

"UR amme? Waaht et b? Rufus George asked him. ["Your name. What it be"?]

"It's, it's, its Victor. Wilber answered.

"icter, ats a cood ammm." Rufus George said, then added, ot no une ith at ammm." ["Victor is a good name."] Rufus George said, adding ["Don't know one with that name."]

∽ Chapter 24 ∾

Mary hurried down the hall to check on Hank, expecting the worst. He had looked so bad when she had brought him to the hospital. As she approached the door, she could hear a strange sound. Her heart skipped a beat in fear of the unknown of hearing the sound coming from her son's room.

She stood at the closed door and listened intently.

It was a chant she heard; yet, it sounded like a song. The words she could not understand and were not like any other she had ever heard. A musical chant, Blue Sky sang rhythmic words while standing at the head of Hank's bed. Mary did not understand, but she knew Blue Sky did.

Mary took a step back and closed the door. Nothing could have helped her more, just knowing everything possible was being done for her son. Also, the many prayers she, Toby, and the girls had prayed for Hank. The other thing on her mind was the sight of Hank. He had been covered with something.

Mary went back to the room where her daughters were sleeping in. She decided not to tell her daughters what she had just witnessed.

∽ Chapter 25 ∾

The following afternoon Paul was allowed out to play. He was told, "Fifteen minutes play time."

He jumped off of the last two steps and landed hard on his hands and knees. He jumped up with no time for pain. Paul ran around the fence and stopped at the spot where Wilber had dug the hole under the fence. Wilber had closed it up so well Paul could not tell where the hole had been

Paul ran around the yard again and again looking for the short fat man. He started looking out in the tree area beyond the closed up hole.

Then it was time for Paul to go in. Rose was watching him as he stumbled up the cabin steps, and as he got to the door his mother was holding open for him, he was yelling breathlessly, "He not there; he not there."

"Paul, who, wasn't there?" Rose's voice was louder than usual.

"Man, the man that dug the hole, Mommy," Paul answered, showing signs of a two year old being upset.

Henry and all of his brothers were working at the oil drilling wells. Rufus George was also there at the oil sight, building the oil hauling wagon.

Rose needed Henry. She asked Inga to go immediately to bring Henry home to the cabin.

Henry saw Inga first. He didn't know whether to laugh or be scared. Inga hardly ever left the cabin and never the yard.

Henry could see this rather large woman running toward the oil drill. She had removed her apron and was waving it up over her head while her body jiggled in places that usually would not move in an entire day.

"Henic, Henic. Rose waits on you." Her voice had a desperate sound in it.

Henry did not waste any time getting back to the cabin.

Rufus George paid no attention and was busy putting the wagon together. He saw nothing out of the ordinary. He did not hear Inga's message.

Rose opened the door for Henry and tried hard not to upset Henry, but she was beginning to believe Paul was telling the truth. They needed to find out.

Henry and Rose drank coffee while patiently waiting for Paul to wake from his nap. He woke wanting to be held and cuddled. Rose talked to Paul asking him to tell his father the story he had told her.

Going out in the backyard meant only playing for Paul. But to his mother and father this was most serious. They all walked around the fence and no one said a word. Henry and Rose watched Paul closely. He walked a little then he skipped and slowly started to hop. He stopped and stood looking down at what was the closed up hole under the fence.

Henry dropped to his knees and Rose knelt down slowly as her body was growing larger each day.

Henry leaned down close to the dirt and could see the outline of the hole and his hand reached out and removed the dry grass, making it very clear and very real what had happened here. This was real and it had happened.

Slowly Henry stood up and reached down to help Rose to her feet. The two stood looking at each other and the realization of seeing the outline of the hole and knowing Paul could have disappeared. This was more than a warning. This was the act of a sick man determined to hurt one of Henry and Rose Donlin Helgens' family. Fear of losing Paul was sickening to them both.

Henry and Rose took extra time putting the children to bed. Inga read each child two of their favorite books to them.

Inga started down the hall to her room when Henry asked to speak to her.

He said, "Inga, no one is to leave the cabin tomorrow. Paul is not allowed out at any time no matter how he begs. Henry's eyes were staring at her without blinking.

Inga's only reply was, "No one will be allowed out at all."

"Rose is going back to the hospital at sunrise to help Blue Sky take care of Hank. You will be in charge of my children." Henry said, before going to Rose.

Inga knew nothing more needed to be said.

ᥴ᠍ᢌ Chapter 26 ᥈ᢒ

Wilber rested most of the day with his foot and leg wrapped in a cheese cloth. Rufus George had helped many plantation workers late at night. Wrapping wounds and caring for men beaten by their owners. It was all done late at night in the dark.

The day's work for Rufus George was over, and he felt happy for getting the new wagon done for Henry. But something else was also on his mind. He began to think of a memory when he was a boy on the plantation. His memory of it had never been forgotten, and now it returned so clearly.

The cotton picking season was long and hard work. All of the slaves had worked so hard that day, and as they trudged home, the sun was almost down. It was such a welcome relief from the hot sun. They could walk slowly and talk as they liked.

Rufus George could hear his mother humming as she always did at the end of the day. To him she was so beautiful and strong. She was the one who kept the group of plantation slaves well from the beatings and abuse they all had to endure.

Rufus George remembered getting to their shanty first; his hand reached out to turn the latch and the door was already open a crack. He felt his father's large hand on his shoulder stopping him from entering first. His father stepped in, and his mother took Rufus George's hand and stepped in next. Nothing looked different or out of place.

The shanty had one room. A bench held the water pail and at the end of the bench is where Rufus George's mother prepared their meal. They ate at a small table. On the table were their dishes. They washed their dishes after each meal and then returned them to the table, not having any place else to keep them. Rufus George's mother hand washed their clothes in a large tank in the same water with all the other slave families.

A blanket hung from a board across the ceiling. It was where Rufus George's father and mother slept. Rufus George slept on a straw mattress pulled out from under his parent's bed and placed each night away from the hanging blanket.

Rufus George was an only child. He learned years later, his mother could not bear any more children. She told him the desire to have another child was always with her. She did not want him to be alone.

The plantation had many acres and needed many slaves to work the land. The other slave couples had large families. When each baby was born, his mother was called on to deliver the baby. If the baby took all night to be born, she still needed to get to the field in the morning. If the baby was coming in the morning, she had to ask the plantation owner to stay with the slave until the baby came and then go to the field.

She also told him the joy she felt was getting to hold the newborn, if only for a few minutes. It somehow took the longing away for a while.

The shanty was extremely quiet. Then Rufus George heard what sounded like a whimper. His parents watched as he got down on his hands and knees and looked below the blanket and under the bed. His eyes adjusted to the darkness and in one swift move Rufus George was on his feet. He threw his arms around his mother's stomach and squeezed her tightly.

What he saw was nearly the same sight Rose Donlin Helgens had seen when she discovered Rufus George along the road.

Suddenly with no warning, they heard a pounding on the door and voices coming from outside of the shanty door. Loud angry voices, then they heard the dreaded sound of dogs barking.

With no hesitation Rufus George remembered his mother's exact words. "Lay on my bed, now." Rufus George crawled under the hanging blanket and lay on top of his parent's bed. He quickly covered up his dirty clothes with a patch quilt.

The door of the shanty swung open and four large furious looking men entered. The dogs jumped through the door and were in the shanty with the guards jerking on the chains around their necks. The dog's mouths opened, showing their sharp, dark stained teeth.

Rufus George's mother told him after the men had left, she could see the hate they were feeling on each man's face.

"Who's in here?" the plantation owner yelled.

"No one but my wife and son" Before Rufus George's father could say anything else the owner walked to the blanket, pulled it back and said, "Get out here boy"

"No, no. The boy is sick, and it could be contagious," Rufus George's mother said in a panic voice.

The plantation owner's eyes widened, and he hurriedly stepped back and roughly pushed the blanket out of his way and headed to the door, motioning for the men to follow.

After he was out, he turned to Rufus George's mother and in a mean harsh voice said, "You get him well or he has to leave. I can't have any of my workers sick."

The first look they had of the slave boy, they recognized him as he lived a short distance from them. The night for Rufus George's family was cleaning the boy and caring for his cuts and washing up his blood from under their bed.

Early in the morning Rufus George's father slipped out of his shanty and went to tell the boy's family where their son was, and he also told them he would be able to hide him for a few days.

He firmly spoke to them about the most important thing they could do to save their son, "Not to come to his shanty; the guards are watching every shanty closely. Go to work each day knowing he is being taken care of." With sadness and heartache the family agreed to do this to save their son.

Rufus George's father continued by saying, "I know a family at the next plantation that would take care of him and then send him to another family. We will keep him hidden until our owner forgets about capturing him and having his guards kill him. The plan I have is to take him to the next plantation in a grain feed sack. I will haul the grain and make sure he gets to the family that will hide him. We must all pray."

⌒ Chapter 27 ⌒

Rufus George's mules moved slowly toward Joseph's cabin.

Wilber rested most of the day with his foot and leg wrapped and it was not hurting as it had. Removing the harnesses took longer because Rufus George was more tired than usual. He had worked longer to get Henry's wagon completed. He checked Wilber's foot and leg as soon as he entered the cabin.

"Icker, it ume ooud, u tay ed une mre ay." Rufus George told Wilber as he rewrapped his foot and leg. ["Victor, it some good, you stay one more day."]

Wilber was more interested in what was going on at the Helgens' cabin than about his foot and leg. He tried to question the big black man. But after eating, Rufus George laid down and fell asleep before Wilber learned what he wanted to know.

Wilber decided he would make sure Rufus George was in a deep sleep and then he would sneak out of the cabin. Wilber managed to get off of the bed. His foot hurt after putting on his boot. He took one step and the floor boards were old and dry. The squeak was loud. He stopped and stood still for a minute, then took another step. The cabin was very dark and extremely quiet. The second squeak was louder than the first. He opened the door and took one more step.

Out of the darkness, yet standing right next to him close enough to touch

Rufus George said, "ya eed elp?" ["You need help?"]

"No, no, Wilber answered. "I need to go to the outhouse."

Rufus George scooped him up in his arms and walked out to the outhouse. Wilber stepped into the outhouse and closed the door and was seething with anger.

Rufus George stood next to the closed door, close enough for Wilber to hear him breathing. By the time Rufus George carried Wilber back into the cabin and laid him into the bed and removed Wilber's boots, Wilber decided he would try again the next night. Only this time he would try a different plan.

ᘓ Chapter 28 ᘔ

Dora had searched in every store in the town of Kolveck. She had, starting with the general store, next the boarding house, the stables. She took the steps up to the doctor's office. She knocked loudly while turning the knob and walked in.

The doctor was always blunt with his words and today was no different.

"Dora," he started out saying. "There is something very wrong with your brother Wilber. You know that, don't you?"

Dora thought it's different already knowing it than hearing it said out loud, especially by someone she knew never liked Wilber.

Dora was becoming agitated at the doctor. She said, "Don't tell me what's wrong with him. Tell me what you can do for him."

"Well," he began. "Maybe I can give him a medicine from back East."

"Let me have some now," Dora yelled at him in a stern voice.

"Well," he started again, "Bring him into the office and I'll examine him and see what I can give him."

"No. No," Dora said determined. "I want the medicine now. If you don't give me some I'm going to go home and get my father's revolver and come back and shoot you. Now, give me something for Wilber."

The doctor couldn't get to his locked medicine cabinet fast enough. He opened it, reached for a dark brown bottle and returned to Dora and said, "Dora, you must understand how many a day Wilber can have. Otherwise he will sleep all of the time. And when he wakens, he will be more confused than ever."

Dora reached out and took the bottle from the doctor's hand, turned, walked through the door, reached back and slammed it shut. Never had she ever acted that way before. Something in her mind was telling her she needed to hurry.

The whole town's people were talking, something was wrong with one of the Kolvecks and everyone knew which one it was.

The sun was up long before Dora woke. The days were long and difficult for her. The routine she had didn't matter any more. She left her bed unmade. She left her dirty dishes unwashed. The clothes she took off at night were the same clothes she put on in the morning. Dust was gathering on the furniture.

She sat eating her oatmeal trying to think of where to look for Wilber today. Then Rose Donlin Helgens' kind face appeared in her mind. She would go see Rose this day.

☙ Chapter 29 ☞

Mary lay awake early in the morning waiting for Elizabeth and Sarah to awaken. The girls woke asking their mother if they could go see Hank.

Mary explained they would have breakfast first as she did not want the girls to see Blue Sky or see Hank in his mud pack.

Rose was in Hank's room when Blue Sky asked the nurse to bring in two tubs of warm water. Hank was awake and looking around, not knowing where he was and wanting to get up. He wasn't whining from pain but upset from seeing nothing familiar.

"Let him get up on his own, Rose," Blue Sky said with a smile on her face.

The first tub of water was warm and ready for Hank. Blue Sky lifted him into the tub and Hank's mud pack was washed off. He was then lifted into the second tub. His skin showed pale pink spots, and he was splashing water on everyone close.

Little tears ran down Rose's red cheeks. The joy of seeing Hank recovering was almost unbelievable.

Rose heard a small tap on the door, and then it slowly opened. Mary and her daughters stood waiting to come in.

Blue Sky lifted Hank out of the water and wrapped him in a large blanket and handed him to Mary. She lowered his body to the floor with her so the girls could touch him, too.

Toby had been checking on Mary and her family every couple of hours. Mary was so grateful for his loving concern.

Elizabeth and Sarah was first to realize what a good friend Toby was. He talked to them, he played ball with them.

He was so different. Toby was kind, gentle and he showed how much he cared. It was at this time Mary began to see the difference between Jessie Rocker and Toby. When Mary gave birth to Hank, it was as though Toby was the father. He always helped Mary, and took care of Elizabeth and Sarah. Making sure they had food and were safe.

Toby had entered the life of two women that loved him very much. Maude was like a mother. Mary was a young woman with two daughters who entered his life under very different circumstances. Before meeting Mary, Toby thought he was in love with Rose. But, Rose had fallen in love with Henry Helgens. And after realizing he was attracted to Mary his love for her grew stronger.

Toby came into the room and sat down on the floor next to Mary and his arms encircled the whole family. He gently took her hand and slowly raised it to his mouth and kissed her hand as the girls watched with a look of fascination. Nothing could have surprised Mary more. The comfort was exactly what she needed and she felt it instantly.

Toby said while holding her hand, "Mary, would you and your children marry me?"

Elizabeth and Sarah were so excited and happy. They answered first saying, "Yes, yes. We'll marry you."

Finally, when the giggling and clapping stopped, Mary answered, "Yes, Toby, we'll marry you."

She handed Hank wrapped in his blanket to Toby. Hank reached up and put his arms around Toby's neck, feeling love and comfort.

Mary and Toby were not aware the door had opened and closed. Blue Sky and Rose left feeling this family needed time alone.

Hank getting sick had made the decision easier for Toby to understand it was time, the love and respect he felt for Mary and the love and desire to take care of Mary's three children.

Toby held Mary's left hand and as they all watched him closely, he separated her fingers and held her third finger to slowly put on a beautiful ring.

"This ring," Toby said, with his voice choking up and looking directly into Mary's eyes. "The ring was given to me from Maude to give to you."

Maude had taken her wedding ring off after the terrible accident with her young husband. Even though Toby was not her son, she thought of him as her only son.

Toby began, "If you---

"Oh Toby, It's so lovely and I would like to wear it the rest of my married life to you. I will never take it off."

The girls were both grabbing at their mother's hand to see the ring. The oohs, and "Mommy, it's so pretty," was a wonderful way to start a new life with Toby in it.

∽ Chapter 30 ∾

In the hall outside of Hank's room, Blue Sky turned her head away from Rose. Blue Sky slowly stepped over by Rose, and for the first time Rose saw tears in Blue Sky's eyes. They did not speak, and Rose wondered if the tears were from relief that she had saved Hank's life. Rose had never witnessed a moment like this. Blue Sky was the brightest and strongest woman Rose knew. Blue Sky's ancestors had passed on Indian cures and prevention medicine to her. She used them, each one according to the illness. Blue Sky was a full-blooded Cherokee Indian.

Rose felt regenerated with Hank's wellness or was this, the relief for them both.

The secret had been kept.

∽ Chapter 31 ∾

Dora left the big white house. She was carrying the bottle of medicine wrapped up carefully in her bag. Getting the harness on the team took Dora longer than usual. They acted anxious and nervous. She wondered if they could feel how she was feeling. Each horse stepped in a different direction. Finally, after Dora talked softly to each horse, they settled down enough for her to get on the harnesses.

The ride would take her two hours. Dora spent the time planning what she would say to Rose Donlin Helgens.

The weather was warm with a cool breeze blowing against her face. As Dora moved closer, she wondered if she could do this. After all, she had helped Wilber. She also had permitted him to commit a crime. A crime she was now so ashamed of.

She pulled her team over to the side of the road and knew she needed to think what she would say to Rose Donlin Helgens.

Dora wanted Rose to know the days after Wilber disappeared, she had time to realize she was guilty, too. She had her head down in deep thought when she heard a loud noise.

It was a team of mules pulling a wagon. She looked and then looked long and hard. A large black man was driving the team toward her. The large black man rode with his head down as if no one or anything could break into or disturb his private collection of thoughts.

⨯ Chapter 32 ⨯

Rufus George finished his day's work and started down the trail toward Joseph Higgens' old cabin. He drove his team of mules slowly like he always did. He was not in any hurry except tonight he had someone to think about.

He closed his eyes, and he could see the pain on the face of the folks whose little boy was taken out of and away of the plantation.

The secret list was passed on, by the whispering in the cotton field. The families everyone knew by name and also knew that certain families would be willing to help this young boy. They also knew the risk they would take, if caught, the punishment would be severe.

The boy was taken from one plantation to the next at night. Each move was in a different hidden, resourceful way. When the boy was able to travel, he left the plantation where he had been born. Rufus George's mother had recognized him as a baby she had delivered and watched as he grew, taking care of each of his illnesses.

The large cotton bags were piled high on a wagon, ready to go to the buyers of the cotton. On the bottom between the bags the little boy was placed in hiding.

When the wagon arrived inside the large cotton storage building, the slave workers were all prepared. The boy was surrounded and a bag thrown over him, then carried to the next hiding place. He was put in a corner of the building where the ripped and torn bags were placed until a woman slave would mend them. She no longer could work in the fields because of age or illness. She knew the boy was there. Her hand worked carefully through the bags and touched him. In her hand she had a piece of bread, spread with lard and sugar sprinkled on top of it.

The old slave woman worked long after dark with light from a lantern. Two men came in and carried the bags to the pile of bags for the next day's picking. The bags would be laid over the back of a donkey in the early morning.

Another donkey had large baskets strapped over each side of his back. The baskets held jugs of cold water for the slaves picking cotton in the hot sun.

The boy was placed in one basket with as many jugs as they could fit in. The other large basket had extra jugs in it so nothing would be different, and no one slave would go without water to drink.

At the drink break in the morning, all the slaves gathered around the baskets. The boy was quickly lifted out and told to run down the row they would pick next. The row of cotton was thick with the cotton plants. He was also told to run like his life depended on it. He was to run to the next plantation.

All of the plantation workers, and guards were in the fields. The boy ran to the end of the row and then on through a wooded area.

The next family in the helping line left their food cellar door open. It was left open for the boy. The boy ran as fast as he could to the food cave. The cave was deep, dark, and very cold.

The old black nanny was wrapped in a large woolen horse blanket as she stepped carefully down each step into the cellar. When she took the last step up and out of the cellar, she was not wearing the horse blanket.

She held the front part of her apron full of potatoes for her master's supper. She turned and closed the cave door.

No one had witnessed what she had done while in the dark cave. She had wrapped the little boy tightly up to get warm, and stay warm all night. The food she brought him was hot soup in a large tin cup. After he ate, he covered his head and cried himself to sleep.

After everyone on the plantation left for the field, the plantation owner had one thing on his mind. He wanted his cotton crop out before it rained.

The old nanny lifted the cave door and whispered, "Come now, boy. Come now, boy. You belong to me."

The small boy carried the blanket up out of the cave with him.

The old woman picked him up and hugged his trembling body to her warm large body. She could feel his soiled pants but it made no difference to her. She would take good care of him.

He told the whole story later, how scared and lonely he felt. He missed his own family and especially his beautiful tender-hearted mother.

The large black woman was kind and gentle. She had talked her master into letting a small boy help her in the kitchen. The master agreed. He did not know who the boy was or who he belonged to. He was too busy to care about a small slave boy.

The boy was saved, and he was with a loving elderly woman who treated him as if she had given birth to him. She hugged him frequently.

The boy would survive and live with her for many years. Word was continuously passed on to his family through the secret line, how well he was doing and the love the old woman felt for him.

The folks of the young boy were secretly informed as the days, months, and years slipped by. The secret words were always welcomed by the boy's folks, painful as it was.

Rufus George tried hard to remember about the day the boy returned to see his folks. It was after the old nanny had died. He came home as a grown man. He carried with him the life savings of the old woman.

Rufus George smiled as he thought about [the boy] now a grown man, who had bought the plantation from the very man that beat him and caused him to run and hide in Rufus George's family cabin.

∽ Chapter 33 ∾

The mules were unharnessed, watered and fed. Rufus George walked slowly to the cabin for a night of rest. He lumbered up to his shelter, bent over from pounding nails in boards.

He had prepared supper ahead of time exactly as he did each morning. It would be ready to eat. This morning was different. He'd prepared enough for two.

Wilber was lying quietly as he was when Rufus George had left him in the morning. The only difference, Wilber had been up as close as he could to Rose and Henry's cabin.

"Ictor, am ome," Rufus George said, ["Victor, I'm home."] as he dished up their supper. He acted happy to have someone to talk to and also to have someone to eat with.

Wilber was happy to have something to eat but he was not happy having to talk to a huge black man.

The two men ate at the large square table Joseph's father had made for his family. The lamp was glowing in the dark room. Wilber found it hard to understand what Rufus George was saying. So his part of the conversation was grunting or moaning as if he understood.

"Inished taa aagon vor Henny. Ee eeded vor hoil ta haal ta town. [Finished the wagon for Henry, he needed for oil to haul to town."] Rufus George tried hard to say it slow.

Wilber shot a quick look at him, then said," Does Henry go out to check his cows everyday, at the same time?" then continued before Rufus George could answer. "Does he check his oil wells everyday? Why do the children have to stay in the cabin all day?"

Rufus George listened, remaining quiet without answering for a few minutes.

"Hoow oou oow boout Henny"? ["How do you know about Henry?"] Rufus George had a puzzled look on his face.

"I, I don't know Henry. I heard his name mentioned in town." Wilber realized he had said more than he should have.

In the dark Rufus George's eyes were large and the only thing Wilber could see was the white of his eyes. Rufus George was looking suspiciously at him. Then he closed his eyes to a squint looking as if he didn't believe Wilber.

"Ictor, whii oou aased boout Henny's amily, ["Why you asked about Henry's family?"]

Wilber swiftly pushed back from the table, stood up and limbed badly into the dark bedroom without saying anything more, or answering Rufus George.

⚬ Chapter 34 ⚬

Dora finally brought her thoughts back and knew she was very close to Rose's cabin. It was late in the afternoon, and the sun was slowly going down. She encouraged the team to start to move. She lifted the reins to give them the direction to go.

Starting up the trail to Rose's cabin was so difficult, she wanted to turn her team around and start home where she could hide from all of the trouble Wilber had gotten them into.

After Dora cautiously climbed down from the wagon she tied the team to a post. The fear was almost unbearable for her. She knew how Henry and Rose felt about her and Wilber.

Rose stood at the window looking out over the wrap-around porch. It took her only a minute before she recognized Dora Kolveck coming toward her home.

Both women had so much to lose. Each woman was doing all they could for love. The love was totally different for each one and to each one.

Rose wanted to firmly ask Dora to leave her homestead. But when Rose turned her head slightly over her shoulder, she could clearly see three small children looking out the window directly at her and Dora.

Rose made the decision not to frighten her little children. They had been through so much when their father had disappeared. She took a deep breath and let it out slowly. Then said, "Dora, what are you doing here?"

"I have come to plead with you for help. I have medicine for Wilber if only I could find him." Dora's voice sounded nervous as she said each word.

Rose started out slowly, "We think Wilber has been here. My little boy talks about him. He told his father and me he had seen him."

Dora's mouth opened, and Rose heard her gasp over hearing Wilber was alive.

"When?" Dora took a deep breath and said. "How many day's ago?"

Rose answered, "Two days ago." Then Rose noticed something else. It was so quiet. She loved the outdoors around the cabin. The birds were always so loud and always sounded happy. Now it was deadly still. No sounds at all.

Rose moved her head slowly and only far enough to see Jay, William, Frank, and all of Henry's brothers watching from all around the homestead. Her eyes moved from side to side. One brother was sitting on top of the wooden fence around the cattle pasture. One brother was watching from the stable. One was standing just inside of the barn. Rose could see his large black hat.

Rose was aware Henry was somewhere down in the cattle pasture. She had seen him ride by the cabin earlier. He had mentioned after their noon meal, he was going to check the cow herd.

Rose took a couple steps backward toward her cabin hoping Dora would leave before Henry returned home. Then Rose heard a whinny from a horse. With no doubt in her mind, she recognized the horse's whinny. It was her magnificent horse, and Henry was coming up from the pasture.

Dora broke the silence by saying, "If only you knew how sorry I am about Wilber. How sorry I am I was part of taking Henry from you. I need to find Wilber." Dora repeated again, "I have medicine for him."

Rose took another step backward and then she turned her head. She could see her beautiful horse. Henry was insight of everyone caught in this dismal situation.

Rose almost ran to Dora and stood as close to her as she could get. For the first time in Dora's life she felt the touch of a woman's body carrying a baby inside of it. Nothing had ever affected her like this. She had grown old in a house with a brother who demanded from her all of his life. She knew nothing of love from someone else or real caring from someone. Dora began to cry.

"Please, leave now. Henry is finally well. He is able to laugh and not have bad dreams.

I'll help you. I promise but you must leave. I will come to see you," said Rose.

Dora was caught off guard. She untied her team, crawled upon the wagon and slapped the reins over her team, and started down Rose's lane onto the trail.

Dora had felt Rose's swollen stomach touching her. For the very first time in her life, Dora felt a new life in Rose's body.

Dora had suddenly felt a surge of love of life she had never known.

As the horses started her toward the big white house, Dora's mind took her right back to Rose's homestead. She would never know the love of a man or know what the love a woman feels when she carries the baby of her husband. She had never had a reason to think about anything like this.

Dora looked up to realize she was almost home. Her mind rested while she took the harness off of her team.

She did not eat; she went directly to bed. She lay in bed exhausted from the long trip. Her thought of Rose's body touching hers made her body instantly feel the same wonderful feeling.

Looking past Rose that afternoon, she had seen the three little children looking out at their mother. She too had seen the men watching over Rose, ready to protect her. Dora's mind would not rest and let her go to sleep.

Remembering back when her mother had given birth to Wilber, she was ten years old and did not even know her mother was having a baby. No one told her until Wilber was born, and she woke in the morning to hear him crying. No touching, hugging or kissing. She just grew up and now she was old, lonely and miserable.

Dora drifted off to sleep remembering she had to bring Wilber home.

↶ Chapter 35 ↷

Henry woke hearing Paul saying, "Please, Mommy, please." Paul was begging to go outside.

Rose's reply was, "Ok, Paul. Would you like to ride in the buggy?"

"Yeth, yeth, Mommy, yeth. Can faather go, too?"

Rose hesitated before answering, then said, "Why don't we ask him at breakfast?"

Henry entered the kitchen with a smile on his face.

Faather, faather, we're going fer a ride," said Paul.

"Ok, Paul, but we need to take the little girls along, too, and I would like to take Mommy along."

"Oh, faather, ok. Can we go now?"

"I'll get Mommy's horse hooked up to the buggy. You help mommy while Inga prepares a picnic for us."

The day was warm with a gentle breeze. It could not have been a more perfect day for a buggy ride.

The laughing and giggling, pushing and pulling to be first was so much fun. Henry lifted each of his little children into the buggy and then Rose slipped her arms around Henry while he carefully lifted her up into the buggy beside him. The love they shared for each other was visible to their children and that's what they both wanted.

Henry lifted the reins and the large wheels began turning. Rose had not asked Henry where they were going, but she knew exactly when the buggy turned toward the trail leading to Joseph Higgins' cabin and homestead.

The horse trotted along the familiar trail while the children chatted and jostled each other.

Henry began telling the children this is where Mommy lived for her first five years after coming to Oklahoma City. The old cabin was coming into view, and now the children were yelling and asking, "You lived here, Mommy?"

"Yes, I lived here with a wonderful elderly man whom I took care of," said Rose knowing she would tell the children about Joseph Higgins when they were older, when they could understand what Joseph Higgins had left her.

Henry slowed the magnificent horse down as they rode by the cabin and headed to the creek.

Rose told the children, "Rufus George lives here alone. He sleeps here and comes to work for your father."

Paul yelled, "Mommy, I want to go in the cabin."

"No, Paul. This is Rufus George's home," said Rose.

Unknowing to anyone in the buggy, inside the cabin next to a window, they were being watched. Wilber carefully peeked out of a dirty dark-stained glass window. He made sure they did not see him.

Henry's familiar face was recognized immediately. He felt sure Rufus George did not tell anyone he was in the cabin. Rufus George had no idea who Wilber was.

Wilber hurried to each window to make sure no one came up to the cabin. He tried to think where he could hide in an emergency, relieved he watched as the back of the buggy moved toward the creek.

Henry, Rose, twins two years old Paul and Margaret and one-year-old Myra had a wonderful picnic along the bank of the creek that Rose had swam in and learned to love her private cove. Rose let each child remove their shoes, stand in the water and splash.

Henry told his children when the water was warmer their mother would bring them to the creek and teach them to swim. He knew he would never go into the water ever again.

Wilber anxiously waited to hear the buggy come up from the creek and drive by the cabin. The noise of the buggy startled Wilber. He ran to stand next to a window watching to make sure it did not stop.

He could see Paul sitting on Henry's lap and the two little girls sat on their mothers lap with their arms entwined around each other.

Wilber slid down under the window and sat on the floor. His foot and leg was healed. He could stand and walk as he did before he fell. Now as he sat on the floor going over seeing the Helgens family, he no longer wanted Henry or Rose. He wanted their children.

∝ Chapter 36 ∝

Early in the morning Rose sent word for her horse and buggy to be brought to the cabin. Inga was informed of not letting the children out to play while she was gone. Inga was told to lock all of the doors with the locks that had been placed high on each door far up out of the reach of the children. Rose asked Thomas to bring Pal into the cabin and stay until she or Henry returned home. Everything Henry or Rose could think of was being done to protect their family.

Henry especially remembered how unstable Wilber Kolveck was.

Rose's trip was to the hospital to see Blue Sky. She had mentioned to Rose she needed an examination with a baby on the way. Rose was surprised Blue Sky knew a baby was on the way because she herself had just realized it at the time. The new baby would be born in the coming fall.

Blue Sky was waiting for Rose. The examination took only a short time but the conversation after took much longer.

"Rose," Blue Sky began whispering slowly and softly. "Let's go for a ride. Let's go to the cemetery, we need to talk and no one must hear us."

Neither spoke on the ride. Both women looked straight ahead.

Rose tied her horse to a post at the entrance of the cemetery. They each crawled out and walked in together. They both stopped at a small heart shaped stone. The small-letters were easily visible.

DARLING DAUGHTER
RUBY MORRISON
AND
BABY BOY

"Rose, Mrs Morrison is here in Oklahoma City," said Blue Sky. She is here to see her daughter's grave. She also would like to see Mary's, son only because he is the age of the grandson she lost. " She said to me, she would like to hold him. "

Standing next to Blue Sky on a clear calm day, looking down at a grave stone, the old memories came swirling back so clearly of the night the two baby boys were born to two very different mothers. It joined a mother together with a different son. It also did something else; it joined together Blue Sky and Rose Donlin Helgens in a life time of bearing the burden of carrying a life-time secret.

Rose remained staring at the grave marker.

"Blue Sky, no one must ever find out," said Rose. "Toby and Mary are to be married in a couple of days. We need to convince them to marry tomorrow. He will give all of Mary's children his name, including Hank."

"No one will ever be able to claim him or take him away from Mary and Toby," Rose stated. "I will go into town to-morrow and sign the papers as a witness, of knowing the family, and attending Hank's birth, and naming him: Hank Toby Weaver."

"Blue Sky, you must get them into Oklahoma City tomor-row and to the judge's office."

Rose whispered. "The secret must be kept."

Rose arrived home late in the afternoon. Inga and Thomas had cared for the children. Rose noticed Pal lay on the floor exhausted over the exhilarating playing he received.

Blue Sky made all of the plans including getting Mary's family to the judge's office. She did not hesitate asking Mary to let Hank stay one more night in the hospital so she could watch over him.

While Blue Sky helped Mary get Hank ready for bed, she told Mary how it will be so much better for her children if they had a good man like Toby for a father to care for them. Then Blue Sky added how wonderful Toby would treat her and care for her.

"The judge in Oklahoma City is a good friend of mine," said Blue Sky. The office will be open tomorrow afternoon. Mary, I can help you get the children ready. The nurses here can help you get the girls and Hank ready." Blue Sky was so determined to convince her.

Mary stood silently listening. Then said, "Do you think Toby should be told?" The laughter brought Toby into Hank's room.

Blue Sky took charge and told Toby he'd have to get dressed up tomorrow in the afternoon and go into Oklahoma City to the judge's office. The smile and glow on Mary's face was all Toby needed to know. This was what he had waited for, for a very long time.

Word was passed on from one friend to another. The hospital staff all wanted to help. Plans were put together and each friend of Mary and Toby offered to make their day a wonderful wedding day for them.

Chapter 37

The judge's office was bustling with excitement about a perfect wedding. Mary looked beautiful as a bride. Toby looked handsome as the groom. The girls were dressed in lacy dresses they each had picked out at the general store. Hank was in Toby's arms while the ceremony was preformed by the judge. A large cheer went up when Toby kissed his new wife and then they both kissed Hank, Elizabeth, and Sarah.

Unnoticed an elderly lady entered the back of the room. She stood very still for a few minutes until she could get through the guests to Toby and Mary. She walked up to Mary and asked to hold Hank. Mary looked at her and was ready to hand Hank over to her.

Rose reached Mary at the same time and said, "Mary, do you remember Mrs Morrison? She is the grandmother of the baby boy born the night you gave birth to Hank."

"Oh, of course." Mary's face changed from a happy smile to looking sad and sorry for Mrs Morrison.

Mrs Morrison took Hank into her arms. She kissed and hugged him to her body. She walked to a chair and sat down looking at Hank as if she recognized him. Rose walked along beside her and sat in the chair next to her.

Rose spoke saying, "He is such a good son for Mary and Toby. He looks so much like Mary's daughters did when they were babies."

Mrs Morrison was deep in her own thoughts. She said out loud, in a quizzical voice, "I can't help but think he looks like my daughter." She took a deep breath, paused. Then said, "Why is that?"

Rose was beginning to feel her heart racing. She could feel her face getting red and warm.

Blue Sky had moved closer and heard part of the conversation and could see the look on Rose's face. Blue Sky moved up to Mrs. Morrison and reached down to pick up Hank and take him from her. Mrs. Morrison refused to let him go.

"No, I came a long way to see him. I need or I want to spend time with him," said Mrs. Morrison.

∽ Chapter 38 ∽

Mrs Morrison's life had changed so dramatically. Her husband spent his time out in the barn; it was his way of bearing his grief. Her son left each morning and did not come home until dark.

The home her family had all loved had turned into a shell of a house with no laughter or talking. They would always love each other but it was not the joyous love they had all shared before their daughter and grandson died.

Mrs Morrison did not know who the father of her deceased grandson was. She thought maybe it was the neighbor boy or someone else she had met while working there.

The thought that disturbed her most was if they could have brought their daughter and grandson home, it would have made their home a happy home full of love, laughter and talking again.

Mrs Morrison lowered her head over Hank's head and kissed the top of his head affectionately.

Mistakenly, she said out loud, "If only I could take him home to see my husband and son. They would love him like I do."

Blue Sky knew this had to stop and stop now. She leaned down and asked, "Mrs. Morrison. Would you like to help put Hank to bed? He's been sick and we need to let him get some sleep. I've been asked to take him and his sisters to their Grandmother Maude."

"Yes, I would love to help," said Mrs. Morrison who was so willing.

Blue Sky carried Hank to her buggy and was going to hand Hank to Elizabeth. Before she could, Mrs. Morrison grabbed Hank and held him close.

Maude had hurried home from the wedding to welcome Toby's new family. She opened her cabin door as her guests came in. The girls were always happy to spend the night with Maude. She always treated them with cookies and milk before bed time.

The girls dressed in their night shirts while Mrs Morrison removed Hank's clothes and redressed him in his night clothes. She also insisted she give him a cup of warm milk. She kissed him several times.

Mrs Morrison laid him in the new baby bed Toby had made as a surprise to Mary. It took only a short time, and Hank was asleep.

Blue Sky walked to the door, opened it, looked back at Mrs Morrison and said, in a firm and direct voice, "I'll take you into Oklahoma City to the boarding house."

Mrs Morrison followed her to the buggy with tears falling down her cheeks.

Maude closed her cabin door, not understanding why a strange woman came into her home and put Toby's son to bed.

∞ Chapter 39 ∾

Inga was at the wedding. She was also in charge of Henry and Rose's family. After the wedding and lunch, Henry drove the buggy up in front of the judge's office pulled by Rose's magnificent horse.

Henry knew he would have to help Inga up into the buggy as he had done earlier. Inga tried several times to get up into the buggy with no success. Finally, she let Henry help her. Again he carefully placed his hands and lifted.

It was dark and he hoped his hands were in the right area. A little squeal made Henry jump and he immediately lowered his hands. Once she was up, he gave a small push and she was safe in the back of the buggy.

The ride was wonderful. The stars filled the heavenly skies, with the full moon hanging above them as if they could touch it.

Once in the buggy Paul sat on one side of Inga's lap and Margaret on the other side. Rose held Myra up in the front of the buggy with her. All of the children had played hard at the wedding falling asleep on the trip home.

Turning off of the trail and on to their lane, Henry and Rose both saw him. A man was on their wrap-around porch and in full view. He had his hands cupped around his face looking in the window of the cabin.

Henry slapped the reins over the giant horse, and the buggy lurched forward at full speed. Inga held tight to the twins.

The short, heavy-set man heard the loud noise of a horse and buggy coming toward him as fast as a horse could run. The man turned and ran to the back of the cabin. He jumped off of the porch and also over the fence disappearing into the darkness. He was running through the trees when he realized his foot and ankle were becoming painful.

He limped into Rufus George's cabin and into the room he had been sleeping in. Wilber crawled into bed leaving on his clothes. He pulled off his boots while in the bed.

His only worry was waking Rufus George, but Rufus George was exhausted, snoring loudly.

No one was at the homestead because of Toby and Mary's wedding. Once Wilber found the area was deserted, he had taken his time. He roamed in and out of every building, looking at the possessions of the cowhands.

The cabin was where he really wanted to go. He looked in the window to make sure no one was in the cabin before he opened the door. It was at this time he heard and saw Henry and Rose.

Henry was sure he recognized the man he had spent seven months with as a prisoner. Rose had never seen him but his description matched the man who had disrupted their life.

The buggy stopped abruptly when Henry pulled back on the reins as close to the cabin as Rose's horse could get.

Henry lifted Rose and Myra down first so Rose could get to the cabin door. She quickly opened it for Henry who carried both of the twins. Then Henry returned to help Inga down, getting her out of the buggy was easier than lifting her in.

Henry took care of his family, helping Rose and Inga slip night shirts on each child, put them into their beds and finally covering them with quilts.

Rose begged Henry not to go out and look for the intruder. "We don't know if he's carrying a gun, Henry. We can't take that chance," Rose pleaded. "He could be hiding, and sneak up on you."

Henry was sure Rose was right, and his family was more important than anything else in his life.

A light tap on the door sent Henry hurrying for his gun first before opening the door. He opened it only far enough to see his brother, Jay, standing there.

"I wondered if you wanted me to put Rose's horse and buggy away for the night." Jay said, wondering why Henry had not done it.

"Thanks Jay, we need to get a posse rounded up early in the morning, and you need to send someone into Oklahoma City to tell Sheriff Les to get as many men as possible and come out here early. Some men will have to walk through the tree area and the others will ride. No one is to go into any man's cabin to search. We're going to cover Rose's three thousand areas of land. Tell William to ride to every renter's cabin and tell them we are coming.

"Why? Henry?" Jay raised his voice not knowing what had happened.

"It's Wilber Kolveck. He's here. Rose and I saw him on our porch when we came home," said Henry.

"Henry, are you sure? Someone could get shot." Jay asked, wanting to be sure it was Wilber Kolveck.

"Yes, yes, it's him. I'm positive Jay," Henry answered slowly. "I couldn't make a mistake about this."

"We're going to get him, Henry," said Jay. "No one will quit until we find him." Jay suddenly knew Henry was very serious. After all Henry had seen this man every day, all day long for seven months.

As Rose walked down the hall passed Inga's room early in the morning, she tapped on her door. Within minutes Inga found Rose in the kitchen heating water to make coffee for all of the men in the posse. She also was making extra coffee for men to take along on their search. Inga started setting out many loaves of bread for the men to also take with them.

Rose could hear men's voices outside along with the sound of horses. The first voice she recognized was Sheriff Les as he opened the cabin door and walked in. Henry greeted the sheriff and remembered all the statements Rose had told him the sheriff had said when he had disappeared. Henry wondered if the sheriff doubted him now.

Sheriff Les sat down at the kitchen table as he had done the last time he was in Rose's cabin. Rose set a cup of coffee in front of him as he said, "Tell me all about this man."

Henry answered by saying, "This man is dangerous. He needs to be caught." Henry's voice was sounding like he felt, he was angry. Then added, "I will not give this man another chance to hurt my family."

∽ *Chapter 40* ∽

Blue Sky woke before dawn, hurried to the shed where her horse was tied up in. She slipped the bridle on him and jumped on bareback. The urgency Blue Sky felt sent her horse into a gallop heading to the boarding house in Oklahoma City.

As Blue Sky entered Main Street, the sun was slowly rising. She tied her horse to the railing in front of the boarding house. The street was quiet as no one was up yet.

Mrs. Morrison opened her door wearing her night gown. Blue Sky did not greet her with good-morning. She said, "Why aren't you dressed? The train leaves in an hour. They never wait for anyone."

"I'm not going. I'm never going home again." Mrs. Morrison's tone sounded as sincere as she could. Blue Sky believed her but knew she had to change her mind immediately.

"You don't know what you're saying. Of course you're going home. Your husband and son need you." Blue Sky was trying so hard to convince her.

"No, no, they don't care any more either. We don't talk to each other." Mrs. Morrison had made up her mind. She was staying.

Blue Sky needed a chair to sit down and think this through, but her mind told her she needed to pick this woman up and carry her to the train in her night gown. But, she also knew she needed to get to Rose's homestead now.

"Why does Hank look so much like my daughter? Why? I want to know," Mrs. Morrison cried out to Blue Sky.

Blue Sky said in a very calm voice, "Because Mrs. Morrison, you want him to. You are the only one that thinks that. But I see no reason you cannot be part of Hank's life. Toby and Mary would love to share Hank with you. You also need to bring your husband and son with you the next time you come. Now, please, get dressed before you miss the train."

"Oh, we would love to be part of Hank's life. I know my husband would love him as I do." Mrs. Morrison's whispered. She also knew this was the only way she and her family could get close to Hank. In her mind, Hank belonged to her.

As she was talking, Blue Sky took the night gown off over Mrs. Morrison's head and slipped her camisole over her head quickly then her under slip, and pulled it down. Blue Sky picked up her dress and helped her put it on. The dress was on and Blue Sky had one sleeve of her coat on Mrs. Morrison's arm and was pulling her out of the door.

Mrs. Morrison stepped upon the steps of the train as the whistle blew and the wheels began to move slowly away from Blue Sky.

Relief showed on Blue Sky's face, as she smiled and waved as the train moved away taking a heart ache with it.

Blue Sky ran from the train station to her horse in front of the boarding house. She knew exactly where she was going.

Rose's homestead appeared to be empty. She knocked at the door. A few minutes later the door opened and Rose reached out and took hold of her arm and pulled her into the cabin. The door was locked at once, both locks, one at the bottom and at the top.

Rose poured Blue Sky a cup of coffee, and the two women sat at the kitchen table waiting for the other to speak.

"Rose," Blue Sky said in a soft voice after realizing Rose was displaying the feelings of a great burden. "We must let Mr. and Mrs. Morrison and their son, be part of Hank's life."

"How can we do that without revealing the secret we have been able to keep for so long?" Rose asked.

"All we have to do," Blue Sky said, "Is, invite them to Hank's birthdays and any special occasions. They can stay at the boarding house, and we'll put them back on the train for their home like I did Mrs. Morrison the morning."

Rose laid her head down on the table, and the vision of what had happened to Henry the last time she was expecting a baby came to her.

Blue Sky reached over and touched Rose's beautiful hair. She began to hum and chant over Rose. It was another way Blue Sky used to remove all the evil spirits and thoughts Rose was feeling.

Rose raised her head and said in a sad and anguished utter, "Wilber Kolveck is near. All of the cowhands are out looking for him, including Henry."

Blue Sky rose from her chair. She motioned for Rose to follow her as she unlocked the door, so Rose could reapply the locks. Blue Sky turned and said, "I'll return tonight when it is sundown. Do not be afraid any longer. You will not know I'm here but the good heavenly spirits of my God will bless your cabin and each one in your home to keep everyone safe." Then added, "If you see a small fire a short distant from your cabin, do not be alarmed. I will be praying and dancing to my God."

Blue Sky stepped soundlessly off of the porch and took one jump and landed on the back of her Palomino horse, heading for home to prepare her ritual for tonight.

∽ Chapter 41 ∾

The night was short for Jay. He did not sleep well, he felt guilty and also responsible to get all of the men ready because he had doubted Henry when he told him about Wilber Kolveck. Jay needed to try and make up for it.

Jay told all of the men to have all of their gear ready to leave from Henry's cabin. He asked them to have their clothes and gear right beside their bunks. He wanted no one to be late.

Jay was next in line, younger than Henry, then Frank and then William. Jay felt the need for Frank and William to ride with him. Frank was strong in every sense. He handled a horse better than any man Jay knew. He could ride and rope calves faster than any cowhand Henry had working for him. He checked the cows every day and night, especially for any cow having trouble calving. He was quiet and never lost his temper. He was the kind of man the men always depended on and went to if they had a problem.

William was tall and thin. He was on the move, needing to be busy all of the time. He enjoyed working on the oil wells. He worked with Rufus George. He didn't understand a word Rufus George said. So, the two men used sign language; just motioned and pointed. William loved Rufus George but he also loved to tease him. His favorite thing to do was put up his fists to indicate he wanted to fight. Rufus George was big, slow and a little clumsy. When Rufus George finally put up his fists, William would run around him knowing Rufus George could not move or turn before William was back around him laughing. The other thing that William loved to do was when Rufus George laid down a tool for a minute, William would lean over and slip it away while Rufus George was not looking. Rufus George would begin looking for the tool, and after a few minutes William would hand it to him and laugh. This happened at least once a day and sometimes more.

While getting his own gear, Jay thought about Thomas. He knew he would want to ride with them, too. Thomas was a boy wanting to be a man, and Jay remembered what had happened the last time they had all ridden together. They would all be required to watch over him. If they did not keep him safe, they all would receive the wrath of their mother.

The cook rang his bell for breakfast while the bunkhouse was still dark and all of the cowhands were nowhere near waking up. But the bell was a homemade bell the cook had invented. It started with a high pitched ring, and then it turned into a loud, deep low sound. The bell woke every cowhand in the entire building. They were on their feet before the bell stopped ringing.

Breakfast was eaten in silence, all but for Thomas. He was excited and wanted to talk about the ride and hunt for Wilber Kolveck. He had a score to settle with that man.

"Wilber Kolveck is the man that nearly ruined my life," said Thomas.

The cowhands including Thomas' brothers looked at each other, knowing what he meant but also knowing he was only nine years old. No one was laughing. They all looked down at their plates. They each remembered the raging water Henry fell into and his rescue, by Wilber and Dora Kolveck who kept Henry prisoner for seven months.

Thomas finished his breakfast before any of the other cowhands he jumped upon his chair trying to hurry the other cowhands by yelling, "Let's go."

The cook had finished feeding the cowhands and immediately started packing bag meals. Each cowhand picked up a bag and put it in their saddlebag along with hanging a canteen full of water on their saddle horns.

⌒ Chapter 42 ⌒

Henry and Rose met on the porch behind the cabin to be alone and say good-bye before Henry left. Henry pulled his beautiful wife to his firm body. Henry loved the feeling he had when he felt Rose's swollen figure. The baby was growing in Rose's body. Henry enjoyed how his family was growing. He tilted his head and kissed Rose long and hard while she kissed him back.

The posse Sheriff Les brought out from Oklahoma City was all lined up waiting at Henry's cabin. Jay brought Rose's giant horse along with his own. Henry walked from behind his cabin and stepped across the porch and down the steps. He mounted Rose's horse.

Henry was aware Paul was jumping up and down in front of the window. Henry could read his lips, "Me go, Papa. Me go, too." Henry knew Paul was happiest when he was outside and riding on a horse with his papa, but not this time.

The men sat on their horses waiting for instructions. Henry stood straight up on his feet in the stirrups.

"Men, we do not want anyone injured," said Henry. "We want only to find Wilber Kolveck. No one is allowed to enter any of Rose's renters cabin. You may go into the out buildings but that is all. Every wooded area will be walked through; no one will ride through. One rider will lead all of the horses around the trees. We will go in groups, in different directions and we will go over every acre of Rose's land."

The riders all headed out in a different direction.

Rufus George had been told to check all of the oil wells because everyone else was busy with other work. He always did what Henry told him and never asked why.

Jay, Frank, William, and Thomas rode onto Joseph Higgins' homestead. Thomas was talking about how good it would be if he found Wilber Kolveck. His voice was loud as they all rode by the cabin Rufus George lived in.

Wilber Kolveck woke to hear several voices. He jumped out of bed and crawled to the window where he could hear better. The voices were loud at first so he crawled back to his bed and crawled under his mattress to hide. Then he could not hear anymore. He crawled back to the window and carefully raised his head up to the side of the window. The horses were all down by the coral. The men were going through the buildings.

Wilber was beginning to panic. He was sure they would search the cabin next. His first thought was to run out of the cabin, but he knew he couldn't run fast enough to get away.

He was beginning to breathe rapidly; he felt short of breath. Suddenly his chest began to feel heavy. And then he heard the horses again, they sounded as if they were coming closer to the cabin. He was shaking all over.

Wilber crawled to the blanket hanging from the ceiling separating the smokehouse and cabin. He crawled under the blanket into the small room trying to hide. He squirmed under the chopping table. Because of his size he couldn't get under the table. He crawled to the door, opened it only far enough to see out. He could not hear any horses or any men's voices. He closed the door and crawled back into the cabin. He then decided staying in the cabin until dark was his only hope.

As he crawled, he would stop and listen for anyone near as the floor boards were old, dry and squeaked when stepped on. The horses did not stop at the cabin; they walked by and started up the trail.

Wilber pulled himself upon the bed exhausted. He was being forced to leave and find somewhere else to hide.

⤳ Chapter 43 ⤲

The groups of cowhands were determined every acre that Rose owned would be traveled over and searched.

Jay and his troop traveled slowly, looking in each direction. The day was very kind to them; it was warm with a gentle breeze. Each rider sat comfortably in their saddle. The quiet ride was what each cowboy liked, all but Thomas. He wanted to talk. It was hard for him to be quiet for any length of time.

The first homestead owners were aware they were coming. Henry had sent word to each renter. The family welcomed them with a cold drink of water. The cowhands refused to go into the renter's cabin, even with an invitation, because of Henry's orders.

The first two renters buildings were searched thoroughly, and then it was back in the saddle and heading for the next homestead.

The trail led away from the homestead and into a wooded area. William led all of the horses around the trees while Jay, Frank, and Thomas walked on foot through the trees. The trees were close together and the underbrush and bushes thick. The trees had been there forever.

Frank was first, out in front, trying to make an opening and a path for the rest of the men. Suddenly a shot rang out; everyone dropped down to the rough undergrowth. Jay and Frank crawled together so Thomas was in between them.

Frank whispered, "Who is it?"

"I don't know," Jay answered.

Thomas started to say something and both Jay and Frank said, "Quiet Thomas."

"We have to find out who shot at us," Frank said as he started crawling and moving forward slowly. Jay's attention was on Frank.

Frank whispered, "Stay here. I'll be right back to get you."

Then Jay looked over to tell Thomas to start to crawl along with him, and Thomas was gone. He was nowhere in sight.

"Thomas, Thomas, where the hell are you? You get back here." Jay was starting to talk louder. He moved in the direction of Frank and when he caught up, Jay explained what had happened.

Frank pointed in a direction for Jay to look through the thickness of many trees. An old shanty stood alone. It had been abandoned years ago.

"I've been here before," said Frank. "I saw that shack. I was riding one day, and it was late when I rode by it. I think it was built by a squatter. And then Rose took over Joseph's land, she asked them to leave, but she also told them they could come and work for her. The family that lived in the shack is a renter now. Rose helped them by building their cabin and helped them get machinery to farm with."

The shanty's windows were all broken out and covered with boards. Many of the shingles were missing. The small board roof over the front entrance was leaning toward the ground. The door looked as if it had to be lifted up to close.

The old shack was occupied again by a squatter and his family. The yard was full of children. They played in the dirt, and each one looked like it. The girls all had long straggly hair. The boys wore no shirts. Not one child wore shoes.

A couple of mangy looking dogs ran around the children while they played.

The door opened and four more little children ran out. They had no shoes and the clothes they wore were torn and dirty.

The shack was not fit to live in. The outhouse was a distance off to the side. The door was missing. The children had no problem with it.

The noise Frank and Jay heard behind them was a crushing sound of the underbrush. Frank reached for the gun on his hip.

"It's me," Thomas said. He knew he might get shot if he did not let them know he was coming.

"Where have you been?" Jay was fully agitated at Thomas.

"I just followed the gun sound. He wasn't shooting at us. He was shooting at a rabbit," Thomas was more than happy to tell them.

"How do you know that?" Jay said, doubting him.

"That's him, that's him, carrying a rabbit. It's for them." Thomas pointed to the kids. The man came out from a wooded area so they all could see him clearly.

"I don't think that little rabbit will feed all of the family." Thomas added

Just then a tall very thin woman stepped out of the open door. She waved at the young man carrying the rabbit and gun. Her appearance showed the life she was living.

Her voice sounded kind when she said, "Come on children."

Frank counted, Jay counted and Thomas counted. They all counted ten small children. They all ran to her to follow, skipping and running around her.

Thomas yelled, "Where is she taking them?"

"I'm going to guess they're going for a swim but also a bath in the creek," Frank whispered.

The three brothers were so busy watching the woman and all of her children they did not realize the man had disappeared.

His voice was strong and firm. "You fellas watching my family? You're on my property. I could shoot all three of you."

Frank jumped to his feet with his hands in the air. "No, no, don't do that. We're just here looking for a man. It has nothing to do with you."

"My name is Frank and these are my brothers, Jay and Thomas."

"By the way what's your name?" Frank said, wanting the man to put his gun down.

"You're not here looking for me?" The man said.

"No," Frank answered.

"My name is Harry. My wife's name is Bertha." Harry smiled when he said his wife's name. Then added, "I call her Berta."

"You own this property?" Jay asked.

"No, we just have squatter rights. The cabin was empty when we ran across it one night when we needed a roof over out kids' heads."

"Is that rabbit going to feed all of your kids?" Thomas was hungry and thought he could eat most of it by himself.

"No," Harry said. "Berta and I will eat some left over pancakes."

"We have food." Thomas was so excited. "We'll find William and bring some food back."

When the three brothers found William, he was sitting in the tree area next to the creek watching a whole family of children swimming and playing in the water. They were all wearing their clothes. They were getting their bath and washing their clothes, too.

The children came up out of the water laughing and looking as happy as they felt. Thomas watched as each child came out of the water. Then his eyes watched as a young girl came out. She was small in size yet, tall with long brown hair. She looked straight at him with her dark brown eyes. She smiled at him, and he had no idea why it affected him. He smiled back and didn't know why he couldn't stop watching her. Thomas spent all of his time around the cowboys at Rose's homestead. This was something new to him

She said, "Hi, my name is Katy."

Jay, Frank, and William were watching too. But they were watching Thomas. They also had a smile on their face trying not to laugh. Once Thomas knew they were watching him, he got up and moved away from his brothers.

The children looked long and hard at the western clothes the cowboys wore. The horses with their bright silver buttons and buckles were also fascinating to each child. The children had not seen any other person since leaving their previous home.

Thomas suggested they build a bonfire and heat their food for supper. The rabbit was skinned and cooked over the open fire. All of the food the cowhands had packed for a three day trip was nearly all eaten. The amount of food not eaten was left with the family.

Frank knew what he had to do. He told Jay, William and Thomas to continue searching the rest of the homesteads.

He told them, "I'm going back to talk to Rose."

The ride back to Rose's cabin was fast as Frank made no stops except to water his horse and let him eat grass.

Rose and Inga were busy all day, keeping the children entertained. Rose was also ready with coffee and lunch when any of the groups of cowhands came back from the search.

Frank rode up to Rose's cabin and was welcomed by three little heads jumping up and down in front of the window. Paul, Margaret and Myra were more than happy to see Frank. He picked Myra up while Paul and Margaret clung to each of his legs as he dragged them across the room into the kitchen to have coffee with Rose. The play time ended when Inga walked in the kitchen and asked if she could read to them.

Frank was eager to talk to Rose about the family living in the shanty on her property.

"Rose, do you remember the shack on the lower south forty? The shack is being occupied by a couple and their ten kids." Frank said it all in one breath.

"But Frank, the shack is not fit to live in," said Rose remembering the last family she rescued from there.

"This family has even less. No food or clothes. Their living conditions are not good." Frank was determined to get Rose to help them. Rose sat quietly watching Frank's face. Rose thought he looked so honest and sincere just like Henry. She could tell he wanted so much to help the family.

"Frank, why don't we bring this family here, and they can use the bunkhouse while all the cowhands are out on the trail. Rose hesitated, saying, "Frank, you tell the cook at the bunkhouse to take out all of the cowhands' personal property and move it into the cook's room."

The big smile on Frank's face was evident to Rose she had made the right decision.

The personal property of each cowhand was collected and packed in boxes and taken to cooks small overcrowded room.

The cook reacted in a way Frank knew he would, but Frank was determined to get the family out of the shack before cold weather set in.

❧ Chapter 44 ☙

The next morning the wagon was readied for the trip back to the dilapidated shanty. Frank asked the cook for all the extra blankets he had in his store room. The cook was in a bad mood but gave the blankets to him. The evenings cooled off, and Frank thought the kids would get cold on the trip back to Rose's cabin.

Frank didn't tell the cook about the ten children coming. He only told him about Harry and Berta needing a place to stay. Frank thought he would deal with the cook when he returned with the whole family.

Frank parked the wagon next to the wooded area and tied the team to a tree. Then he began his trip through the heavy congested trees, bushes and undergrowth.

It was late in the afternoon, and Frank knew when he walked into the trees, the light from the sun would be gone. The chances of his tripping and falling over fallen trees and large branches were on his mind.

He moved in slowly, holding his arms out in front of him. Then he felt around and picked up a branch to use to make sure he didn't walk into a low hanging limb. He did well, only falling a couple of times and then when it was completely dark he realized he was just a short distance from Harry and Berta's squatter shack.

Frank sat down next to a large tree truck and leaned back and drifted off to sleep. The trip through the many trees left him needing to rest before starting back with Harry's family. When he woke the sun was coming up.

The first thing he had to do was convince the family to go with him.

He woke with a jerk as two thin, flea-infested dogs were standing over him licking his face with sloppy wet tongues dripping on him. Just behind the dogs were five little children watching and giggling with laughter.

Frank tried to get up and then he realized he couldn't move, he was tied to the tree. The little kids continued to jump up and down while pointing at Frank. Then the two dogs began to bark just inches from Frank's face.

Minutes went by, when Frank heard Harry's voice. "What's going on out here?"

"Ok, kids untie him," said Harry coming upon the scene.

"Sir, the kids were just having fun," said Harry. "I hope your ok."

But Frank thought the smile on Harry's face would burst into laughter any minute.

"No, no, I'm fine," said Frank. "I came to talk to you and Berta."

Frank rubbed his neck where the rope was tied around him. If the kids thought this was fun, he decided right then he did not want to play with them.

"I have something to offer you, Harry," Frank said when they arrived at the shack. He was ready to tell them about Rose Donlin Helgens. Frank sat down on a broken step and pretended not to notice how he slid along to the side, all the while he hoped he would not end up with a sliver in his bottom.

He told Harry and Berta how good Rose would be to them. They would be able to take good care of all of their children.

The couple was very quiet for about ten minutes. No one said a word. Frank was beginning to think they would not go with him. Then Harry spoke and said, "I think we'll take you up on the offer."

Frank jumped up from the dangerous step and said, "My team and wagon are on the outer edge of the trees. If we go now, we'll have a little light to get through the trees. We'll have to carry the small children"

Harry called all of the children and explained they were moving.

Most of the younger children took the news well. The older ones decided immediately they were not going. The yelling began until Harry in a deep loud voice, said, "We are all going to Rose Donlin's homestead. Rose told Frank she would help us. Now, I do not want to hear any more yelling."

Berta told the kids to put on all of their clothes so no one would have to carry anything.

Frank looked at the older ones and had a feeling he was going to pay dearly for even coming here.

The children were all lined up so Harry and Berta could count them. The two littlest children were each carried by a parent. Harry had two more walking with him and Berta did the same, leaving Frank with the four oldest boys.

Frank led the family into the thick overgrowth. He tried to find and use the path he used to get to the shack but it was almost impossible. Frank would holler out so Harry and Berta knew where he was.

The four boys walking behind Frank would disappear and hide behind a large tree. When Frank turned around, they would be gone. Just as fast as they disappeared they would jump out from the trees. The boys were having fun teasing Frank. After all, it was Frank who disrupted their home. They frequently stopped so all of the family could catch up. This was a difficult trip for everyone.

Frank turned around frequently now. Each time one of the boys would be missing. He also realized they were whispering and laughing more. If he turned around fast, they had a big smile on their face. They were planning revenge.

Frank stopped and yelled at the boys to keep up. There were only three.

"Where's he at?" Frank was getting tired, thirsty, and hungry.

One of the boys made the mistake of looking up. Frank looked straight up at the highest branch of a very tall tree and sitting in the crouch was the missing boy. The wind was moving the branches making Frank dizzy watching as the boy could easily fall.

The other boys were not, afraid. They had seen their brother climb trees many times. After all climbing trees was their entertainment. But this time the wind was very strong. Each brother yelled for him to come down. The climb down was slower for him. He knew he was going to be in trouble even if he didn't fall so he was careful. When his bare feet hit the ground he immediately stood behind his brothers.

Frank turned and started again.

The boys whispered to each other. They were not giving in. While they waited for the boy to come down, he went unnoticed that one brother had slipped around and was now ahead of the group.

He held the lowest tree branch back and when Frank was a step away, he let the limb loose to hit Frank. The limb was covered with leaves so Frank didn't see it coming. He lay on the broken limbs and dried leaves with fear as the young boys looked down at him grinning.

"Ok boys, that's enough," Frank said firmly. But they were not done yet. They weren't out of the woods.

The boys offered to help him up. They each grabbed an arm. At the same time something was slipped into his pockets.

Frank was sure they were nearly to the wagon. Then he heard the horses whinny. Relief engulfed his body. He needed to get Harry's family out of the trees and to a new homestead.

The boys reluctantly climbed into the wagon box while waiting for the rest of the family. All of the boys were sitting right behind Frank watching him closely.

Frank sat holding the reins and something felt like it was moving in his pockets, his shirt pockets, and also his pants' pockets. Without looking, he slipped his hand in his shirt pocket and he felt it crawl over his hand. He then knew in each of his pockets a tiny baby snake had been placed.

The one thing in Frank's life he feared the most were snakes.

He knew this was the most important reaction and decision in his life even while his body was feeling terror. Even his breathing had changed. His breaths were coming in little short gasps.

The boys had tried to break him down and make him show some weakness, but he pulled up all of his inner strength he could and lifted the first baby snake out of his shirt pocket and dropped it over the side of the wagon. His body shivered. Then he did the same to each pocket with each little snake being dropped to the ground. When he was finished, he wanted to vomit but again, he would not let himself give in.

The boys were very quiet. They bowed their heads. Each boy turned his head while looking down and looked at each other. They were planning their next move.

Harry got to the wagon with his three children. The little ones were scratched and crying. Berta was right behind with her three children and everyone was extremely tired. They all hugged each other and kissed each other and cried. They were so happy to see their whole family together. This was the first time they had ever been separated.

The four older boys sincerely showed they cared about their little brothers and sisters. They each tried hard to comfort them. Frank could not believe what he was seeing after what they had put him through. What he had not seen was the boys each had the saddest eyes. They believed their family would never be the same.

Frank moved the wagon out slowly as the little ones were quieting down from a terrible ordeal of tripping and falling. Harry and Berta hoped this was worth the pain of trying to get a better life for their family. The scratches and cuts would be taken care of at the Higgins Hospital. Frank thought about Rose, and he would also notify Blue Sky.

The staff at the Higgins Hospital was overwhelmed. Each child was given special care. Blue Sky came with all of her loving spirits to help a family in need.

Frank waited patiently until the whole family had been seen and treated for. He would deliver them to the bunkhouse where each bed had clean sheets on and there was enough food so no one would ever be hungry again.

The cook had been alerted to get food ready for a big home-coming. Frank had not informed him yet.

Frank witnessed Harry holding Berta in his arms, and they were both crying. Their lives were about to change, and they hoped it would help their children most of all. That's the only reason they agreed to come. They had no idea who Rose Donlin was.

⟶ Chapter 45 ⟵

Wilber welcomed the darkness. His biggest fear was waking Rufus George. He knew exactly where he was going to hide. He quietly got out of bed and down on to the floor. He waited a few minutes. Then he crawled across the floor to the blanket, crawled under the blanket to the smokehouse door. He continued to crawl until he was outside. It took him a couple tries to get up on his feet.

Going around Henry and Rose's cabin was very difficult for him. He wanted to look in Paul's bedroom window. Just one more look.

He was a small distance from the homestead when he saw light in the windows of the bunkhouse. The noise he heard was voices of children. He needed to get closer.

But something else caught his attention. He saw a small fire. He needed to get closer. He could see someone by the fire.

Wilber crept along on his hands and knees. The sight he saw was someone he had never seen before. The person was dancing around the fire and saying words he had never heard. It was so frightening to him. He wasted no time getting to his feet and started toward his new hiding place away from the Rose Donlin Helgens homestead.

Wilber did not stop until he had reached his destination.

The cellar door was not locked. He was as quiet as he could be on unsteady feet. The basement was so dark but he reached the last step and knew exactly where he was going. He opened the door to a room he had never forgotten about but had hated as a child. This time no one was pushing him into the room and closing and locking the door on him. Dora would sneak down to the punishment room and bring him food and something warm to drink. He always cried when Dora came in the room and she would wipe away his tears, each time. If she had time she would read him a story, depending on how long their parents would be gone.

The bed was made up with old quilts. Wilber slipped his boots off and got into bed with his clothes on. Within minutes he was sound asleep. As bad as the room had been as a child, it now was his survival. He had found his hiding place.

His sleep changed as the old nightmare began. He was little again and it was so real. He felt the same exact feelings as he had when he was locked in the room. He imagined he saw giant spiders and big bugs on the wall. The loud voices he heard were only in his head. And, they were his mother and father yelling at him, and sending him to the punishment room.

The room was always cold and damp. He would close his eyes and cover his head with quilts to try and escape his torture.

Wilber woke the next morning feeling sick to his stomach. He had not eaten since eating breakfast with Rufus George the morning before. The storage room with fruit and vegetables was next to his room in the back of the basement. The jars sat on selves for the winter months. It was not winter, but Wilber needed to eat. He now had food for a long time. If he could not remove the lids on the jars, he would break the jar to get the food.

Wilber had everything he needed. Except the one thing he wanted, was one of Henry and Rose Donlin Helgens' family.

...story to be continued...

Frank sent the cook into Oklahoma City to purchase the food for the big homecoming. The cook had not been told about Harry and Berta's ten children living in the bunkhouse. The cook's life was about to change.

Rose decided she needed to go to the bunkhouse to meet Harry and Berta, and their wonderful children before she made her trip to visit with Dora Kolveck. The children's actions were more than she expected. They were used to being free.

The groups of cowhands returned after searching Rose's three thousand acres.

Wilber was not found.